A few words from
Ben Westin, Laura's Ex:

Laura thought I was too old-fashioned. Little things, like the way I kept track of my auto-body-shop business in a spiral notebook, drove her nuts. Now I actually have one of those fancy-schmancy computers. Not only has it made my work easier, it's introduced me to one heck of a woman—through some kind of on-line network thing for singles.

I don't know her real name, or what she looks like. I only know that I'm falling in love with a complete stranger.

Dear Reader,

How To Flirt. How To Boost Your Self-Esteem. How To Make Him Fall In Love With You. How To Lose Twenty Pounds In Twenty Minutes. Just a few headlines from fashion and beauty magazines—bibles for some women, waiting room fluff for others. I'm a devoted fan.

And so is Lilah McCord, a single mom who's had it with staying home alone on Saturday nights, in Cait London's supersexy novel *Every Girl's Guide To...* She studies articles on seduction, on being a "now-woman," on...*something* rough-and-rugged Clint Danner later uncovers in her apartment. Ever see a cowboy blush?

One way to ensure a blushproof romance is to date a man without meeting him. Laura Westin, lonely divorcée and title character of Toni Collins's terrific *Un*happily *Un*wed, falls in love via a computer singles network with a complete stranger—or so she thinks.

Next month, look for two Yours Truly titles by Dixie Browning and Kasey Michaels—two more entertaining and engaging romance novels about unexpectedly meeting, dating...and marrying Mr. Right.

Yours truly,

Melissa Senate
Editor

P.S. Please write me with your opinion of Yours Truly novels. I'd love to know what you think.

Please address questions and book requests to:
Silhouette Reader Service
U.S.: 3010 Walden Ave., P.O. Box 1325, Buffalo, NY 14269
Canadian: P.O. Box 609, Fort Erie, Ont. L2A 5X3

TONI COLLINS

Unhappily Unwed

Published by Silhouette Books

America's Publisher of Contemporary Romance

SILHOUETTE BOOKS

ISBN 0-373-52006-9

*UNHAPPILY UN*WED

About the author

I can't remember a time when I *didn't* want to be a novelist. As early as the third grade, I can recall being hauled off to the principal's office because I was caught writing short stories in class. The best grade I ever got in high school was for a short story about wacky time travelers written as a special project in history class. I wrote my first novel when I was seventeen, but it took me another eighteen years to get published. Perseverance pays!

I was born and raised in St. Louis, where I still live with my rather unusual extended family—my teenage son, who stopped calling me "Mom" when he was six; my mom (I still call her "Mom" because I want to go on living); a German shepherd who has a love-hate relationship with the mailman; a bad-tempered parrot and a rather large potbellied pig who thinks I'm her mother.

*Un*happily *Un*wed is Toni's seventh novel for Silhouette books.

For Charlotte, Linda, Karen, Shirley,
Mindy and the rest of the gang
at Magna Bank's Mackenzie Pointe
Banking Center, for making it
look like so much fun....

And especially for Christina Ann DeLuca,
who definitely makes it more
fun for *me!*

1

Their divorce was the nastiest Fowler Falls had ever seen. This came as a great surprise to most of the residents of that small Wisconsin town where they'd grown up and spent all of their lives since. Everyone in Fowler Falls thought they were an *adorable* couple. They were like Barbie and Ken—trim, blond Laura, the popular homecoming queen and straight-A student, and Ben, dark, handsome, all-American jock. How many of their friends and neighbors had described them over the years as "cute"? Maybe they were, when he carried her books home from school when they were in fifth grade, and maybe even when he took her to their senior prom...but toward the end, they were anything but adorable.

But the good folks of Fowler Falls still saw those two as best friends walking home from school when they looked at them, even though it had been a good twenty-five years since he'd carried those books, and over seventeen years since he'd taken her to the senior prom in that beat-up old heap he called an automobile. The whole town had attended their wedding, after all. That was the way it was when you grew up in a small town. Everybody knew everybody else, and everything about everyone else. Most of the time it could be a blessing.

Other times, like now, it could be a curse.

Laura Westin frowned at the thought. She'd always loved the laid-back life-style of Fowler Falls. It was home and always had been—but lately, whenever she returned for a visit, she found it harder and harder to deal with the questioning looks she got from the locals when she went to the grocery story or stopped for gas. Even worse were the blatant inquiries from the elderly ladies who had nothing better to do than poke their collective noses into other people's business.

No one in Fowler Falls had understood. Least of all her ex-husband.

That was the problem.

"Excuse me?"

Laura's head jerked up. Her executive assistant, Zara Kimball, was standing in the doorway, looking at her apprehensively. Zara didn't look like the thoroughly competent executive assistant she was, with her punk hair—bright red at the moment!—and funky clothes. Though the powers that be at the bank had made a monumental effort to "do something" about her appearance, Zara had persisted in the expression of her individuality—and Laura steadfastly refused to replace her.

"What?" Laura asked distractedly.

"Didn't hear me, did you?" Zara asked, though her tone made it crystal clear that she already knew the answer.

Laura shook her head. "I'm sorry, no," she confessed. "I didn't."

"You've been on a different planet every day this week," Zara observed wryly.

Laura smiled wearily. "And what planet have I been on?" she asked, keeping her tone as light as she could manage.

Zara shrugged, "I don't know—but I know it hasn't been Earth," she said with certainty.

"That obvious, is it?"

"Like a billboard smack in the middle of Times Square," Zara told her.

"They say time heals all wounds," Laura said weakly.

"That's just a load of rubbish 'they' tell those of us who are going through garbage because 'they' don't know what else to say and think they have to say something," Zara snapped. "Personally, I'd rather 'they' didn't say anything if they couldn't come up with something more constructive."

"Those of *us?*" Laura asked, not missing the way Zara had lumped them together. "You?"

"Yeah—me," Zara said with a nod. "You seem surprised."

"No—yes!" Laura nodded. "Yes, I am. I mean, you don't—"

"I don't act like somebody who's been burned?" Zara laughed. "I put up a real good front, that's all. And I have my network."

"Your what?"

"My network—my computer network," Zara explained. "It's a group of people who talk via computer—sort of like the pen pals of the nineties."

"I see," Laura said. But she really didn't.

"I've been communicating with a group of singles like myself, people who are divorced or have been in bad relationships. It's better than group therapy."

"And cheaper, I'll bet," Laura concluded.

"Significantly."

"Sort of like a group gripe session?"

"Absolutely. You should try it sometime."

Laura shook her head. "Thanks, but no thanks," she said too quickly.

"You never know unless you try."

"I can imagine."

"It's a lot of fun."

"I'll just bet it is."

"You might actually like it," Zara told her.

"I doubt that."

"I met a guy."

"I'll just bet you did."

"Well, I didn't actually *meet* him," Zara confessed. "We've been communicating, and it's been great. On-line, you can be yourself. You don't have to worry about how you look or any of that superficial garbage. It's the safest form of sex currently available."

"Safe sex," Laura repeated with unmasked amusement.

"Sometimes the communications get pretty racy," Zara told her.

"I'm sure."

"Really," Zara said insistently. "Because you don't really know the other person—that is, know them in the Biblical sense. You can be as open as you choose."

"And you can encounter all kinds of crackpots," Laura pointed out.

"That's the beauty of it," Zara insisted. "They don't know who you are. They don't really know where you live. You can reveal as little or as much as you want about yourself. It's freedom."

Laura frowned. How could she communicate her feelings—with or without a computer—to complete strangers when she hadn't been able to do so with her own husband?

"For you, maybe," she said aloud.

Zara made a face. "How'd you get to be so cynical?" she asked.

"My husband—my ex-husband, that is—gets most of the credit," Laura said darkly. "I stopped believing in fairy tales the day he told me being a successful banker meant I had to be a lousy wife."

It was the truth. Until that day, she had believed anything was possible. She'd believed in miracles. She'd believed she had a good, solid, happy marriage. She'd had no idea her husband didn't feel the same way until they renovated their first house—the first house they had ever owned—and were about to move into. He talked about watching their children grow up there, about the life he wanted to share with his family, his wife. A life she'd made clear she didn't want.

And he told her he wanted a divorce.

He'd had better days.

Better, definitely, but not too many he could consider worse. On the Richter scale of bad days, this one had been a 9.5, he decided as he put the Closed sign in the window and headed for home.

Ben Westin owned the only auto body/customizing shop in Fowler Falls, so business was almost always good. There were days it was *too* good. He had just two men working for him—and they were his brothers, Sam and Ray, so they could take days off without fear of finding the infamous pink slip in their pay envelopes. Or so they thought. After today, holding down the fort by himself with six jobs to be completed and his two employees off fishing, Ben was ready to fire both of them. They knew better. If they couldn't be more responsible, he thought, annoyed, he would just have to find someone who was.

Still, putting in long hours at the shop was better than the alternative—going home to the big, empty house he'd almost shared with his wife and the family he'd once believed they would have. Spending the evening alone didn't appeal to him at all. The marriage hadn't worked, but that hadn't been his fault—or had it?

He'd known Laura all his life. They'd grown up together. How could he *not* know that she was ambitious, that a job, a life here in Fowler Falls was never going to be enough for her? How could he not know that their marriage wouldn't be enough for her? No—he *had* known. But he'd loved her too much to take a chance on that love being strong enough to hold her. But then . . .

Can't think about that now, he told himself. He'd already rehashed it in his mind so many times. What was the point? he'd asked himself, frustrated. It came down to one very large question, one to which he might never have an answer: How could they have known each other for so long, yet not really know each other at all? No, there was no point in dwelling on it. It wouldn't change what went wrong between them.

Parking his customized pickup truck in the driveway of the big house on the edge of town, the big house the whole town had turned out to welcome them into, he found it impossible not to think about his ex-wife, about how happy they'd been when they first bought it, how much fun it had been to renovate it, make it totally their own. He could still see Laura painting their bedroom, getting more of that deep rose paint on herself than she did on the walls . . . hanging the flowered curtains and refinishing the big four-poster bed that would be covered in the same floral

print with which she'd done the curtains . . . filling the
room with family photos and other items of senti-
mental value. Ben frowned. Even before the divorce,
most of the time it was empty—and lonely, as was the
rest of the house.

He wondered what his ex-wife's bedroom in Chicago looked like. He'd seen Laura's high-rise apartment on Lake Shore Drive, and it was definitely
befitting the vice president of one of the Windy City's
largest banks. Sleek, modern, expensive. That was
Laura. That was Laura now, but it hadn't always
been. Laura had grown up a small-town girl, in a
modest home like the one in which he and his brothers had grown up, on the same street. It had been
enough for him, but not for Laura.

Ben went into the kitchen and made himself a couple of thick sandwiches, then parked himself in front
of his home computer to do his bookkeeping. The
computer Laura had urged him to buy. Back then,
he'd resisted the idea. It wasn't something he would
have bought for himself. He didn't even want it when
she suggested it—he told her he wasn't mechanically
inclined, or whatever it was people were called when
they were good with computers and could program a
VCR. But he'd learned to use it and keep the shop's
records and books with it. Still . . . he would have tossed
it into the trash on more than one occasion, had it not
proved so useful to his business. It made the record-
keeping process so much easier and more efficient.
The salesman who'd sold it to him had taught him to

use it, and he was surprised at how simple it had been, once he learned the basics.

Now, as the screen came to life, he paused to consider the main menu for a moment. There were still things he hadn't tried. He hadn't needed to. All he ever used it for was his work. But now... now, he found himself considering the options. This particular software had all sorts of possibilities. Like the ability to roam the local networks, the discussions on the bulletin board services. These options had never interested him before, but tonight he felt the need to interact with another human being—even if it *was* only on a computer screen.

He went to his modem and dialed on-line, finding himself in a "room" with a group of newly single parents who, like himself, were lonely and frustrated. There was Lonely in Landview, whose husband had left her for his secretary, who, it turned out, was very pregnant at the time. And Hopeless in Highland, who had been married three times and taken to the cleaners in each of the divorce settlements. He was considering bankruptcy as his only hope of salvaging anything.

"I'm convinced each of my exes had the same lawyer," he wrote. "That shark has X-ray vision when it comes to my wallet. He can figure out to the penny how much I have, then he asks the judge to give it to his client."

This was depressing, Ben decided, but stayed on the line. He called himself Misery Loves Company.

"My ex and I were like Barbie and Ken," he typed, remembering how many times he'd been told just that by the good folks of Fowler Falls. "We grew up together, lived on the same street, went to the same school, knew all the same people."

"And she left you for the boy next door, right?" responded Hopeless in Highland.

"Wrong," Ben typed. "I was the boy next door. She left me for a bank in Chicago."

"Interesting." This was Hopeless in Highland.

"You think so?"

"Well, yeah. Most of us get dumped for other men. I don't know anybody who got dumped for a bank."

"The bank is where she works. It's her job. She's a V.P., makes a lot of money," Ben responded.

"In that case, I hope you asked for a lot of money."

"I didn't ask for a dime." Ben was indignant.

"Are you nuts?" Hopeless wanted to know.

"The jury's still out on that one, I think."

"I disagree. Men are ripped off in divorce cases every day of every week by women wanting large alimony payments. It's about time women had to pay, too. They want equal rights, don't they?"

"Well . . . yes."

"I rest my case."

"You sound like a lawyer."

"Bite your software!"

Ben smiled to himself as he contemplated a response. This was more fun then he had ever thought it could be. . . .

* * *

"So, can we expect you this weekend?" Laura's brother, Nick, was calling to see if she would be attending yet another family get-together in Fowler Falls.

As uncomfortable as those trips usually made Laura, she'd long ago accepted them as a fact of her life. Nick wasn't one to take no for an answer.

"I don't know, Nicky—"

"You do this every time I ask, Laurie," he responded.

"Do what?"

"Drag your heels," he told her. "I extend the invitation, you try to worm out of it. I keep pressing, and in the end, you show up. Why don't you just say yes right off the bat and save us both the trouble?"

"You know why," Laura said.

"Because of Ben, you mean."

"Yes."

"You don't have to see him if you don't want to," Nick insisted.

"So you keep telling me."

"You don't."

"Then why is it I always *do?*" Laura wanted to know.

"Chance."

"Chance, my foot!" Laura snorted. "Fowler Falls is so small, I can't even stop for gas without running into at least one of the Westin brothers."

"That's stretching it just a bit—"

"That's not stretching it at all. In fact, if I didn't know better, I'd think the whole town had shrunk over the years!" she shot back at him.

"Besides," Nick went on, ignoring her comment, "it shouldn't bother you to see him."

"How do you figure?"

"You *are* divorced, sis."

"Precisely."

"So why do you care what he does or where he goes?"

"I don't."

"Then why should it bother you to see him?"

Laura, too tired to argue, finally surrendered and promised to be there. "You won't be sorry," Nick told her.

"So you keep telling me."

And so he did, she reflected as she hung up. Nick was happily married with four children. How could he possibly understand how painful it was for her to come home, to see Ben and know things would never be right between them again?

Yes, Laura dreaded the weekends—those she spent at her brother's home in Fowler Falls, anyway—because she hated what was always a confrontation between herself and Ben. Why couldn't their divorce have been a civilized, friendly one? And if it couldn't be, why couldn't she avoid running into him on those visits?

She frowned. The answer was a simple one: There was still too much feeling between them. They weren't one of those couples who could divorce and be good friends afterward.

There was too much history there, Laura thought miserably.

She looked at the huge brass wall clock as she returned to the living room. It was getting late and she was exhausted, but she did have a couple of things she really needed to do on the computer. She had a 9:00 a.m. meeting and wouldn't be able to do them at the office first thing in the morning.

She dragged herself to her desk in the far corner of the room and switched on the computer. After a half hour of trying unsuccessfully to work, she found herself considering the local networks Zara had raved so much about. Curiosity made her decide to check them out—heaven help her if Zara ever found out!

After roaming for a short while, she found herself in the middle of a bulletin board discussion in progress among a group of divorced parents. Hopeless in Highland was lamenting the sorry state of the legal system and three failed marriages that had left him financially destitute—except, obviously, for his modem and computer!—and Misery Loves Company, clearly as new to this as she was, was baring his soul. He must have been married to a real shrew, the poor guy, Laura thought sympathetically.

She introduced herself into the discussion, identifying herself as Unhappily Unwed.

"Nice software you've got there, Unwed," came the response from Misery Loves Company.

"And how would you know about my software?" she typed, smiling to herself. It was a strange feeling, flirting with a computer.

"Has it been that long? Don't you recognize a pick-up line when you see one?"

"Is that what you're doing, Misery? Trying to pick me up?" Laura laughed as she typed.

"C'mon, Unwed, give me a break! Can't you see I'm new at this?"

"Oh, I can definitely tell," she typed. "But then, so am I."

"Gee. Does that mean we're a couple of—"

"Don't say it, Misery. There are others present."

"Oh, right. I almost forgot." Good thing she couldn't see him blushing.

"Oh . . . one of those."

"Now what does that mean?"

"You shoot from the hip, I'll bet," she guessed.

"That's what my ex-wife used to say about me."

That's it, Laura—stick both feet in your modem the first time out. "Sorry about that," she apologized.

"No harm done. That's probably the only thing she ever got right about me," he admitted.

"Let me guess. You two barely knew each other and rushed impulsively into a marriage that was a mistake before the ink was dry on the marriage license," she concluded.

"Not exactly. We knew each other forever. We just didn't really know each other."

"I hate to tell you this, Misery, but that doesn't make a whole lot of sense," she told him.

"My divorce didn't make a whole lot of sense."

"Really? It would seem we have a great deal in common."

"Then perhaps we should continue this discussion privately," he suggested.

"And just how do you propose we do that?" Laura wanted to know. Surely he wasn't suggesting a face-to-face meeting. After all, they didn't really know each other. They were just two faceless characters on a computer screen.

"We don't have to use the bulletin board. We obviously both have the necessary equipment."

"What do you suggest?"

The suggested specifics appeared on her screen almost immediately. *Not a bad idea,* she thought. "All right," she typed quickly. "Tomorrow, then?"

"Same time, same place."

2

I don't believe I really did that.

Laura thought about it as she lay awake in bed that night. For all her scoffing and skepticism, she'd not only checked out the networks and bulletin boards, she'd actually made a contact with someone. With a man. *He seemed nice enough,* she told herself. *But was he really? He could be the great faker of all time.*

After all, Ted Bundy fooled a lot of people.

Still, as Zara says, it's safe as long as it's via computer, she reminded herself. *He doesn't know where I live. He doesn't even know what I look like.*

It could be fun, at that.

Fun. How long had it been, she wondered now, since she'd done something just for the fun of it? She couldn't remember. She'd devoted herself so totally to her career for so long, she'd forgotten what it was like to do something, anything, just for the fun of it.

Laura frowned. How many times had Ben told her just that?

He'd accused her of being a workaholic. He said her career was the only thing that mattered to her. It wasn't true, of course. Her career was important to her, yes—she wouldn't deny it—but no one else had been able to understand. Not her husband, not her brother, not her parents, who still lived in Fowler Falls, had been married over forty years and were as traditional as it was possible for a couple to be. No one had been more stunned than her parents when she announced that she and Ben were getting a divorce. Her father told her what a terrible mistake she was making. Her mother confessed that she would never be able to understand how she could leave a wonderful man like Ben for a *job*. Her mother had never understood that her work wasn't just a job.

Nor had she understood that the breakup of their marriage didn't mean that Laura had stopped loving Ben. Laura hadn't been able to make her believe that regardless of how they felt about each other, they simply couldn't make their marriage work. As much as Laura had loved Ben—still loved him—it hadn't been enough.

Maybe, she reflected now, he hadn't loved her enough.

I don't believe I really did that.

Ben couldn't sleep, couldn't stop thinking about his conversation, such as it was, with Unhappily Unwed. He'd never believed he would even try such a thing— that was the sort of thing that would be popular with

Yuppies, not with a down-to-earth country boy like himself.

He wondered if it was the sort of thing Laura might experiment with.

No, he thought with certainty, *it's not her stuff. She may be a successful Chicago banker now, but she's not into that sort of thing.*

Unless she's changed. And she has definitely changed.

If she hadn't changed so much, they would still be together. He didn't doubt that for a minute. They'd been so right for each other—when they were kids, when they were in high school, when they were first married. How could two people so right for each other drift so far apart?

He'd never been able to figure that one out.

In the beginning, their love had been enough. It had been enough for both of them—more than enough. But then, Laura's needs had changed. They could no longer be satisfied in Fowler Falls. They could no longer be satisfied by him, by their marriage.

Why? he asked himself. *Where did I fail her?*

He looked at the framed photographs on the wall—photos taken of the two of them over the years. There was one of them at the tender age of seven, walking home from school—at an age when most boys thought of girls as having "cooties," he was clutching her hand protectively. Then there was one of their first date—a couple of skinny, awkward-looking kids, her with braces and him with a mild skin problem. By the senior prom, he thought as his gaze moved to the next photo, they'd both blossomed.

Their wedding photo once hung to the right of the prom photo. It was no longer there because Laura had taken it with her. Why, he wasn't quite sure. *She didn't want the marriage,* he thought bitterly, *so why did she want the wedding portrait?*

She'd told him repeatedly that she did want the marriage, but her actions were speaking a whole lot louder than her words at that time. If their marriage was so important to her, why was her career occupying almost all of her time? He'd been anxious to start a family—but she was seldom home, and when she was there, she was usually too tired to make love.

Ben frowned. Until she got that promotion, the physical side of their relationship had been wonderful. He remembered what making love with her had been like...

"We're going to be late for work, you know," he told her.

She gave a low, throaty laugh. "We could always live on love," she suggested.

"I don't think it'll pay the bills," he said, nuzzling her neck. He loved the feel of her, from the silkiness of her hair to the softness of her skin to the way their bodies just seemed to fit together, as if they were made for each other.

"It won't put food on the table, either," she said lightly, "but I'll bet I end up gaining weight."

"Let's hope so," he responded without hesitation, knowing exactly what she was referring to.

She wrapped her long arms around his neck and kissed him with a passion they'd had for each other since they were teenagers necking in his father's car.

"Let's make a baby," he urged her.

She hadn't responded, Ben remembered now, which had led him to believe she was at least agreeable to the idea.

How wrong he'd been.

She always insisted she *did* want children—"but not right away," as she put it so many times. Her career was just getting off the ground, she was working such long hours. It was always something.

Then it was too late.

Laura decided against telling Zara about her network experience.

Bad idea—very bad idea, Laura thought as she rode up to her floor in the crowded elevator. *She would never let me hear the end of it.*

She particularly wouldn't let her forget it was her idea if anything important developed because of it, either.

Laura almost laughed aloud at herself then. *Listen to yourself—"if anything important developed because of it"! As if anything could!*

She still wasn't convinced of that.

She saw Zara chatting with a group of secretaries at the water cooler as she disembarked from the elevator. "Hi, boss!" Zara called out, greeting her with an energetic wave.

Laura cringed inwardly. She hated it when Zara called her "Boss"—especially when she did so in front of the other secretaries—but she hadn't been able to break her of the habit. It made Laura uncomfortable, but she wasn't exactly sure why.

"Are those letters typed?" Laura asked.

"I finished them before I left last night," Zara replied.

"The fax to San Francisco?"

"Already sent."

"The interoffice memos?"

"Distributed."

"What time did you come in this morning, anyway?" Laura wanted to know.

"Seven-thirty, as I always do. Why do you ask?"

Laura shook her head. "No particular reason," she said, but to herself she replied, *Now I know why I hired her. She's the perfect secretary.*

Almost perfect, anyway.

If only she looked more like a secretary and less like an avant-garde painter. But then, she thought with an injured sigh of resignation, one couldn't have everything.

Look at me, she thought sadly.

She went on to her office. The first thing she did after seating herself at her desk was check her daily planner to see what the day's schedule looked like.

Not much going on today. Good, she thought, not feeling up to a full day. It had been a long night, and she was exhausted. She frowned. Toward the end of her marriage, she'd had a lot of nights like that.

All of them, in fact.

She glanced at the computer on the right-hand side of her desk and wondered idly what Misery Loves Company was doing right now. *Wouldn't do any good to try to get him on-line now,* she thought. He had a career of his own. She couldn't remember if he'd told her that or not—maybe she'd just assumed it—but she had the definite feeling he wasn't sitting around his keyboard, waiting for messages.

Tonight, she told herself. *I'll contact him tonight.*

Her curiosity was definitely piqued. As long as she really wasn't putting herself at risk, why not contact him, learn more about him? What harm could it do?

It might even be fun, Laura decided.

"Hello again, Misery!"

"That you, Unhappy?"

"That's 'Unhappily,'" Laura corrected.

"Is my screen red, or what? Sorry about that typo!"

"Apology accepted."

His response was slow in coming. "Know what? Once I get past the initial B.S., I'm not sure what do do next."

Laura smiled to herself. "I suppose we could start by telling each other a little about ourselves."

"Sounds good to me. What's your sign?"

"Very funny."

"Isn't that the line used for pick ups in bars?"

"I wouldn't know. I've never picked anyone up in a bar," she told him.

"Neither have I. But I do watch TV."

"Aha—a couch potato!" she responded.

"Not really."

"No?"

"No. I will, however, admit to being a part-time couch potato. Usually on weekends, and especially in winter. I come from a small town, and there's not a whole lot to do when the weather's bad," he came back.

"Really? I grew up in a small town, too, but it seemed like there was always something going on there, any time of the year."

"I guess it just depends on what small town you're from."

"Maybe."

"It was different when I was a kid. I never ran out of things to do," he recalled.

"Maybe you should think 'Young at heart.'"

"Whaaaat?"

"My ex-husband and I grew up together in that small town, and we used to do a lot of fun things together. But it was as if the day he turned twenty-one, all of those fun things ceased to exist," she answered.

"Sounds like my ex-wife." A grumble?

"Oh? In what way?" she wanted to know.

"She was one of those high-powered executive types. There were a lot of things I would have liked to do, but I wouldn't have even suggested any of them to her," he confided.

"Why not?"

"I guess because I figured she wouldn't be interested anyway. It just wasn't her style."

"What wasn't?"

"Skating on the pond outside town, sledding, snowball fights—that sort of thing," he typed.

"Oh, that sounds like fun. I wish my ex had wanted to indulge in a bit of child's play."

"Sounds like we were pretty much in the same boat."

"Right—the *Titanic.*"

"Do you have any kids?"

"No. Do you?"

"No—but I wish I did."

"I feel the same way—now."

"Now?"

"I married young. I wanted a family. I wanted kids. But I always thought there was no hurry, that we had plenty of time."

"What about your husband—ex-husband, I mean?"

"He wanted a baby for our first anniversary. And the second, third, fourth and fifth."

"Well, at least you had a spouse who wanted kids."

"Yours didn't?"

"That's an understatement. She wanted a career—first, last and foremost."

That brought back memories—but not pleasant ones. It made her think of all the arguments she and Ben had had over that same issue.

"You objected to your wife having a career?"

"No—just to it being her number-one priority, taking all of her time."

If Laura didn't know better, she would think she was talking to Ben. But Ben wouldn't use a computer even when she'd tried to explain to him how beneficial it would be to his bookkeeping at the shop. He wouldn't be caught dead on a network or a bulletin board. She started to type again....

"Sometimes it requires a substantial investment of time and energy to get a career in any field off the ground."

"Sure—but once she became successful, I thought she'd slow down."

"She didn't?"

"If anything, her work demanded even more of her time."

Laura frowned. She felt a great deal of sympathy for him, for his predicament.

Ben would be amazed.

Ben *was* amazed.

The lady clearly had a career herself, yet she seemed to understand. She knew how *he* felt. But more than that, she understood; she didn't declare him unreasonable for feeling as he did.

The word *sexist* was never mentioned.

Why, he asked himself again, couldn't Laura understand? Why couldn't she see how he felt? Why didn't his feelings matter to her?

He frowned. She would probably ask why *he* couldn't see how *she* felt, why *her* feelings didn't matter to *him*. Toward the end of their marriage, they'd lost that necessary ability to communicate, which had once come so easily to them.

Why? He still didn't know the answer to that one.

He didn't want to think about Laura—it was still too painful. Yet, he couldn't seem to help it, especially now. There was something about Unhappily Unwed that reminded him of Laura, though he wasn't sure exactly what. Was it because she was also a career woman whose career ruined her marriage—or did it go deeper than that?

There were times that the opinions she expressed, phrases she used, sounded just like Laura. If he didn't know better, he would think she was Laura—but then, a computer network wasn't Laura's style. Oh, she would use a computer to take care of business—how many times had she urged him to do the same?—but not for her social life. That just wasn't Laura.

He wondered now if Laura was seeing anyone these days. They'd been divorced a little over a year now, and separated longer than that. Laura was a young, attractive, vital woman.

Of course, she was also a woman who, much like the nuns, was married to her work.

If she *was* seeing anyone, Ben concluded, it would have to be one of those uptight, buttoned-down executive types. These days, that description probably fit all the men she came in contact with. Sophisticated, successful—he suspected that was the kind of man she really wanted anyway.

The thought of Laura with anyone else made Ben's blood boil.

Laura wondered if Ben was seeing anyone.

She thought about it as she stood at her bedroom window, staring into the night, the brilliant lights of the Chicago skyline spread out before her. Normally, she enjoyed the view, but tonight she paid no attention to it. She was thinking about her ex-husband, about what he might or might not be doing with his free time.

If he was seeing someone, Laura wouldn't be surprised.

He certainly had his share of female admirers, she remembered. *Shirley, the waitress at Ned's diner, or Pam, that bottle blonde who does the manicures at the beauty parlor. Or Sylvie, down at the market—she did everything but plant her behind in his grocery cart.*

Rumor had it the single women in town had thrown a party the day the divorce became final. While there wasn't a shortage of single men in Fowler Falls, there *was* a shortage of single, attractive personable men.

In fact, Laura thought, *there are only three now—Ben and his brothers.*

She told herself if he *was* seeing someone, it was none of her business. *Why should it bother you?* she demanded of herself. *You're not married to him anymore!*

But it *did* bother her.

It bothered her more than she would ever admit to anyone except herself. *I never wanted the divorce,* she thought bitterly. *Ben never understood that—or maybe he just didn't care—but I didn't.*

She wasn't looking forward to the weekend, to going home. Going home meant that, sooner or later, she would be running into her ex-husband—and she would leave Fowler Falls feeling even more miserable than she was sure to be when she arrived. It was a pattern she'd become accustomed to.

Reluctantly.

"Do you keep in touch with your ex?" Ben queried.

"Are you kidding?"

"Bitter divorce, I take it."

"To say the least."

"He fought the divorce?"

"Not at all. He wanted it."

"You didn't?"

"No. I believed our problems could have been worked out."

"Something else we have in common. My divorce was the last thing I wanted."

"Didn't you try to stop it?"

"I figured there wasn't much point in fighting the inevitable—she was going to leave me anyway. Better to make it a clean break, a legal one."

"That's basically how I felt. We had grown so far apart, it would have taken a miracle to keep us together."

"Love wasn't enough?"

"Not for us, unfortunately."

"Like I said, something else we have in common."

"Did you ever tell your wife you loved her?"

"All the time."

"No—I mean at the time of your split."

"At that point we weren't doing much talking at all, of any kind. We'd even gone way past shouting."

"I'm sorry."

"So was I. What about you?"

"What?"

"Did you hand out a lot of 'I Love Yous'?"

"Not at the end."

"Why not?"

"I didn't believe my feelings for my husband really mattered to him."

"I guess neither of us had anything left to salvage."

"I guess not."

Ben stared at the screen for a long time. He and Unhappily Unwed seemed to have so much in common, but he still didn't feel ready to throw caution to the wind. The disintegration of his relationship with Laura had made him wary of all women. As connected as he felt to this woman, he still had reservations about revealing his name to her, telling her where he lived.

Not yet, he told himself.

"Are you still there, Misery?"

"Yes—just got lost in thought for a minute there."

"I know the feeling."

She seems to know an awful lot about my feelings, Ben was thinking.

Should I tell him or not? Laura wondered.

She was comfortable with things just as they were between herself and Misery Loves Company. Very comfortable, in fact. But she wasn't yet ready to make a full confession, tell him her real name, where she lived, what she did for a living—specific things, identifying things.

He seems like a decent fellow, she thought, *but then, my judgment hasn't exactly been the greatest when it comes to men.*

He was right about one thing: they did have a lot in common. The most important thing they had in common was their respective failures at marriage. They'd both married their first loves, and they'd both been deeply disappointed. Neither had wanted to give up on their spouses, neither wanted their marriage to end in divorce.

If only Ben had felt that way, she thought.

Her on-line conversations with Misery Loves Company had unearthed a lot of memories. That night, she did something she hadn't done since she left Fowler Falls. She took her wedding album out of the closet and spent the rest of the evening looking at it.

It seems as though it were from another lifetime, she thought sadly.

They were so young then, so young and happy and in love. No one who had attended their wedding would have believed then that their marriage would end in divorce.

She wouldn't have believed it herself.

She wouldn't have believed Ben would be so willing to give up on her, on them. It would have never occurred to her that he wouldn't allow her to grow within their relationship, pursue her own goals and ambitions.

He'd always been so supportive—even when we were kids, she recalled. *But times change, people change. Ben and I just changed too much, moved in opposite directions.*

She frowned as she looked down at a photograph of her taken in the bride's room at the church, where she'd prepared for the ceremony. The photographer had captured her in her wedding dress, standing before the full-length mirror, gazing into it as though it could show her what the future held for her.

If only it could have, she thought, flipping the page. The next photograph brought tears to her eyes.

It was the one taken of her and Ben making their vows.

3

—⟶—⟵—

"You heard me. The answer is no. Out of the question," Ben said crossly. "I don't think I can state it any more clearly than that." He looked menacing, his stance firm, his expression a scowl, wrench in hand as if it were a weapon to be wielded.

"But, Ben—" Sam began, unwilling to surrender just yet.

"What part of 'no' didn't you understand?" Ben wanted to know, his tone unmistakably angry. He continued on about his business, checking out the pickup truck that was brought in that morning for extensive bodywork after one of those rare major traffic accidents in Fowler Falls.

Sam tailed him, unwilling to give up. "It's just one day, Ben," he said, his tone pleading. Normally, Ben understood these things. But it was clear to Sam that this time he didn't.

Dropping the wrench suddenly, abruptly Ben turned on him. "It's always been 'just one day' with you, Sam—Ray, too. Last week it was 'just one day' to go to that fish-off, or whatever it was. Monday, the bass were biting so well that you two just *had* to go out to the lake for the day. If you two could make a living fishing, you'd be in Hog Heaven.'' He wiped his brow with the back of his hand in a gesture that stated his annoyance more clearly than words ever could, then drew a deep breath. ''Look—I don't mind you two goofing off when things are slow around here, but when we're as busy as we are now, I expect both of you to be here, putting in a full day's work.''

Ben started to return to his work, dismissing his brother with a shrug, but Sam refused to be dismissed. ''Then we can't even take half a day?''

Ben rolled his eyes skyward, exasperated. ''What did I just say?'' he demanded hotly, wanting to put an end to this and get back to work.

Sam frowned, ''No.'' he conceded.

''And what, exactly, do you think that means?'' Ben asked.

''No?'' Sam guessed, clearly hopeful that Ben would correct him.

''Bingo. Now get back to work.'' Ben gestured sharply with his thumb, indicating that the topic was no longer open for discussion.

Ben drew in a deep breath as he watched his brother shuffle away. It had to happen, sooner or later. *Might as well be now,* he told himself. *Might as well get it over with.* It wasn't good for business. That was how he justified that moment of nastiness. He had to think of the business—and so did they.

If he were to be totally honest with himself, though, he would have to admit that he was taking out his private frustrations on Sam and Ray, that his unusually short fuse had less to do with his brothers' goofing off than it did with his own feelings of helplessness and failure where his marriage was concerned. No matter how hard he tried, Laura was always on his mind. Never very far from his thoughts. Unfortunately.

Why now? he asked himself. *It's not as if we separated last week, or even last month. No...it had been much longer than that.* There were times it seemed like another lifetime.

It's been a while—so why now?

He knew the answer even before he asked himself the question. It was because of Unhappily Unwed.

Sharing his thoughts and feelings on divorce—his divorce, specifically—was something he'd never done before. He had never even discussed Laura and what had gone wrong between them with his own family. Whenever anyone *did* ask, all he'd ever said was, "It just didn't work out." It was nobody's business, after all.

He'd never been *able* to talk about it before because he never could bring himself to admit he'd failed, that he hadn't been able to hold on to his wife, keep his marriage together. A part of him still believed it was somehow his fault, that he'd been inadequate as a husband.

But with Unhappily Unwed, it was different. Boy was it different! It was like confiding in the local bartender, or maybe even a psychiatrist, someone you didn't have to live with or even see every day. Unhappily Unwed didn't know his real name, and he didn't know hers. She didn't know where he lived or what he did for a living. For now, he wanted to keep it that way. He wasn't quite sure why, but he did.

What she *did* know, what mattered most, was what it was like to be divorced, to be stuck with a divorce he'd never really wanted, to lose someone he'd always thought he would be with forever. She knew because she'd been there herself. It wasn't his own private hell; it had been hers, as well. She understood his pain and frustration as only someone who'd been there themselves ever could. She could share his pain because she'd experienced it firsthand. She'd known the feelings of loss, of hopelessness.

She understood him better than Laura ever had.

"So what shall we talk about tonight, Misery?"

"I don't know. What do you want to talk about?"

"You're leaving it up to me?"

"Sure. Why not?"

Laura sat there for a long moment, staring at the blank screen, carefully considering her options. Pursing her lips thoughtfully, she mentally composed her response. Finally, she reached for her keyboard and started to type again, feeling a bit whimsical.

"Playing shrink with me, are you?"

"What gives you that idea?"

"For one thing, you're leaving the topic of conversation up to me. For another, you almost always answer a question with a question."

"Doesn't mean a thing."

"Sure. Was that your secret ambition, Misery—to be a shrink?"

"If I could treat only women."

"Oh?"

"Think about it. All those women, looking to me for help with their sexual problems."

"What makes you think all of their problems have to be sexual?"

"This is my fantasy. Besides, shrinks almost always find sex at the root of their patients' troubles."

"You've been watching too much TV, Misery."

"Think whatever you like—but everybody knows patients always fall in love with their therapists."

"Which just proves how troubled they are. Is that why you want to be a shrink—to take advantage of vulnerable women?"

"I never said I had a secret yen to be a shrink. You did."

"Then what would you be? If you could be anything in the world you wanted to be, I mean."

"Anything at all?"

"That's what I said."

"A stuntman."

"You mean like in the movies?"

"That's exactly what I mean. I've always loved those old Burt Reynolds movies—you know, *Smokey and the Bandit, The Cannonball Run,* stuff like that."

"You and my ex-husband."

"He wanted to be a stuntman?"

"Not that I know of. He did love car-chase movies, though."

"Most men do, I think."

"Wonderful—sports and car-chase movies. The macho national pastime."

"I guess it is a male thing."

"Fortunately for women, most of us are immune."

"You've never had a yen to run amok?"

"Can't say that I have."

"What's your secret desire, then? What's the one thing you've always wanted to do but never dared?"

"You're so dramatic—are you sure you never wanted to be an actor?"

"Stop stalling. I 'fessed up—now it's your turn."

Laura was hesitant. He was asking her to tell him something she'd never, ever told anyone—not even Ben. She wasn't sure she *could* tell anyone. He would probably laugh—but then, even if he did, she wouldn't know it.

Or would she?

Here goes nothing, she thought as she started to type again. At least she would never have to face him—not if she didn't want to.

"All right. But you have to promise not to laugh."

"I promise. Scout's honor."

"All right—I wanted to be an Olympic gold medalist," she confided.

"In what?"

"Figure skating."

"Why'd you think I'd laugh at that?" he wanted to know.

"I don't know. I just did. I thought everyone would laugh."

Everyone had laughed, she recalled now, when she first took up skating. They'd teased her about wanting to be the next Peggy Fleming, unaware that she *did* have such ambitions.

"Everyone?"

"When I was young, I loved to skate. All of the kids in our town did. During the winter, that's just about all we did on the weekends. But when I was skating, I would daydream—I'd see myself in some wonderful, exotic place like Switzerland or one of the Scandinavian countries, skating before an international audience and panel of judges. Having hundreds of red roses thrown on the ice at my feet. Nobody knew it then—they still don't know—I used to sneak out at night so I could skate alone and fantasize. It was exhilarating!" she remembered.

Laura braced herself, waiting for his response, certain it would come in some form of a joke. When it finally did appear on the screen, when she saw that it wasn't a joke, her whole body sagged with relief. Maybe there was someone who understood, after all.

"That's not silly. Why didn't you ever tell any-one?"

"I felt silly. I thought they'd laugh." *I was sure they would,* she thought, recalling how her friends had teased her.

"Even your husband?"

"Especially my husband." He had been the worst of the lot, she remembered.

"Why?"

"It was so inconsistent with the way my family and friends and even my husband—ex-husband—saw me. I knew they'd never take me seriously."

"You're sure about that?"

"Believe me, I'm sure."

She thought about it. She *was* sure, very sure. They *had* laughed—all of them. Especially Ben. He hadn't understood, they hadn't understood. How could they, after all? They didn't see her in the same way she saw herself.

They never had.

"Want to talk about it?"

Ben sat in the kitchen of his parents' home in Fowler Falls, the home where he and his brothers had grown up, facing his mother. His mother, a woman in her late fifties with graying hair, seemed, as she always had, to be not only at home there, but a part of the kitchen. Maybe, he thought, because most of her time had been spent there when he and Sam and Ray were growing up. Maybe because whenever he thought of her, he thought of her there. *Didn't everyone* think of their mom that way? Emily Westin knew him too well, always had. No matter how hard he tried to hide anything from her, as a child or as an adult, she could always see through him. *Why do I even try?* he wondered now.

"You could tell?" he asked, genuinely surprised.

Emily smiled patiently, speaking with the wisdom of the ages. "Maternal instinct," she offered as an explanation as she poured him a second cup of coffee.

"That simple?" he asked, brushing a lock of hair back off his forehead nervously.

"That simple," Emily said with a nod of assurance, patting his hand in a comforting gesture.

"Do all women have those instincts?" he wanted to know. He was genuinely interested. He would have been willing to bet Laura didn't. She just wasn't the maternal type.

His mother shook her head. "No, I don't believe they do," she answered honestly, only too aware of how many women couldn't care about kids—even their own. "But those of us who really love children, really want them, have a special bond with our babies from birth."

He didn't respond. He was thinking about Laura, still wondering if she had any maternal instincts. He didn't see how she possibly could, given her disinterest in having any of her own.

Somehow, he doubted it.

"Do you want to talk about it?" Emily Westin repeated. How like her, he decided. Always there for her sons when they needed her, no matter what.

Ben frowned. She couldn't help him—no one could. "There's not much I can say on the topic that hasn't already been said," he answered.

"Laura," Emily guessed with a mother's special clairvoyance.

He nodded. *Wouldn't do any good to lie,* he told himself. *It never had in the past anyway.*

"Have you ever told her that you still love her?" his mother wanted to know.

Ben sighed. "What good would that do?" he asked, his tone grim.

"It might accomplish a great deal—you never know." She cut a large slice of chocolate cake, put it on a plate and placed it in front of him.

"I doubt that."

"Given how you still feel about her, don't you think it's at least worth a try?" Emily asked. His mother knew—actually, the whole town knew—how much he'd loved her, how brokenhearted he'd been since the divorce.

He looked down at the cake but didn't take a bite, even though chocolate was his favorite and he never, ever refused it when offered. "My feelings aren't the problem, Mom," he said finally. They weren't. they never had been. He'd never doubted *his* feelings for *her.*

Emily looked at him questioningly, waiting for him to go on.

"What's kept us apart isn't how *I* feel—it's how Laura feels," he said. "Or, more accurately, how she doesn't feel."

"You're saying Laura no longer cares for you?" There was a note of disbelief in her voice, and more than a little doubt in the expression on her otherwise compassionate face.

"I don't see how she could. Remember she wanted the divorce." Why did she have to even ask? he wondered. Laura's actions spoke volumes.

"But she hasn't actually told you she doesn't care anymore," Emily concluded. She gave him that look—the one she'd always given her boss when she felt they'd acted unfairly.

"Well, no."

"Then you're just making an assumption," Emily concluded.

"It doesn't take much in the way of guesswork, Mom," he said grimly. "She made it pretty clear that she wanted that job in Chicago more than she wanted me or our marriage." She'd said she wanted both, actually. He was the one who'd felt it was necessary to choose.

"Wanting a career doesn't necessarily mean she doesn't love you or want to be your wife," Emily said gently.

"A husband and children were always enough for you." He remembered quite clearly how content his mother had been in her traditional homemaker role.

"I come from a different generation, Benjamin," she reminded him. "When your father and I were first married, a husband and children were all any woman wanted."

Ben looked down. "It's not just Laura this time," he finally admitted. He needed to talk to someone—who better than his own mother?

His mother gave him a quizzical look but didn't say anything. For once she didn't know what he was going to say before he actually said it.

"I've met someone—sort of." Now that he brought it up, how was he going to explain it?

"How can you 'sort of' meet someone?" Emily wondered aloud.

"I've been corresponding with a woman over a computer network," he explained. "We've never actually met face-to-face."

"Then she's more like a pen pal than a love interest?" Emily Westin was clearly trying to make some sense of her son's so-called new relationship.

"For the moment." He could only hope she didn't ask where it was going, since he didn't know himself.

"Meaning?" She obviously was going to ask—where could he go from here?

"Meaning I don't *know* where this is going—yet." He wasn't even sure it *was* going anywhere. He wasn't even sure it was a relationship.

"Do you plan to meet her?" Emily wanted to know, unable to hide her surprise that he could be interested in someone who wasn't Laura.

"I hope to at some point," he told her. "She's an interesting lady, that's for sure. She certainly understands me better than Laura ever did." Laura hadn't understood him at all, but his mother probably wouldn't believe that.

"Don't go getting involved with her or anyone else until you're over Laura," his mother warned. "It can only hurt the woman—and you."

Ben frowned. He understood that only too well. He'd already been hurt enough for one lifetime. He had no desire to experience that kind of pain again.

Besides, he'd never deliberately hurt anyone the way Laura hurt him.

Laura was intrigued.

She found herself wanting to know more about Misery Loves Company—things such as his name, what he looked like, where he lived, what else they had in common besides their divorces. She was intrigued by this man of mystery with no name, no face, no identity other than a bunch of words on a computer screen.

What she really wanted to do was to meet him.

"Would I love to be able to read your mind!"

Startled, Laura's head jerked up. Zara stood in the doorway, wearing black leather pants and a bright red shirt that almost matched her hair. Her earrings were large gold hoops, and she wore several gold bangle bracelets. "What?" Laura asked, not having heard her the first time.

"I said I'd love to be able to read your mind now," Zara said, crossing the room to place some mail in Laura's In box. Her bangle bracelets clattered with the movements of her arm.

"You'd be bored to tears," Laura assured her. She wasn't about to tell Zara what she'd really been thinking. She knew only too well what a bad time her assistant would give her.

"I don't think so," Zara said with a sly smile. Nothing got past Zara Kimball. That, Laura conceded, was what made her such a perfect assistant.

"Oh? And what makes you say that?"

"The look on your face." Zara didn't miss a beat—unfortunately.

Laura wondered what kind of expression she must have had on her face when Zara walked in. "It's not what you think," she insisted, though she doubted Zara was buying any of it.

"Oh, yeah? What *do* I think?" Zara asked in a half-teasing tone. Her bright red curls bounced with the shake of her head.

"Knowing you, you probably think I was thinking of a man," Laura guessed.

"Is that what I was thinking?"

"Isn't it?"

"Of course. Isn't that what *you* were thinking?"

"Not at all."

"Yeah, right."

"I wasn't."

"Have it your way. Was it by any chance your ex-husband?"

"Zara—"

"All right, I get the message. You've got that meeting at two," Zara reminded her, starting for the door. But the look on her face said Laura hadn't fooled her at all.

"I haven't forgotten," Laura assured her. How could she possibly forget?

She hadn't, but her mind was on other things right now. Things Zara would have loved to hear all about but would never let Laura hear the end of.

No...she couldn't tell Zara about Misery.

She hadn't told anyone about him. No one, except perhaps Zara, would understand. They would think she'd really lost it, having a relationship—such as it was—with a man via computer. Or they would think she was desperate, since she hadn't been involved with anyone since the divorce. Most likely they would think she was desperate. Just what she didn't want them to think!

Haven't been involved with anyone—I haven't had so much as a date! she thought ruefully.

But then, she'd gone out of her way to discourage the men who *had* been interested in her. She hadn't wanted anyone who wasn't Ben.

Did she want Misery? That was a question she couldn't really answer at this point. She was certainly fascinated by him. There was no question that he understood her better than any man she had ever met. She wondered what kind of woman would leave a man like him. The same kind of woman who would leave a man like Ben, she concluded.

Probably a real shrew, she decided. *Only a shrew wouldn't be able to live with him.*

"Hey, Unhappily, do you like animals?" he wanted to know.

"That depends. Just what kind of animals are we talking about here?" she asked.

"Animals. You know, Unhappily, pets. Dogs, cats, birds, fish, snakes."

"Snakes? No snakes, Misery. Dogs and cats, yes. Birds and fish, yes."

"But no snakes."

"No snakes. Why do you ask?" she questioned.

"Just curious," he answered.

"That's all?"

"That's all," he assured her.

"I take it you're an animal lover," she guessed.

"Yeah. Animals are good at sizing people up. They know a good egg from a rotten one."

"What?"

"They can't be fooled."

"In other words, if I were a phony, your dog, Rover, would know it," she typed.

"If I had a dog, Rover, yeah," he said.

"Even via computer?"

"Well, no."

"Do you think I'm a phony, Misery?"

"No. Why do you ask?"

"You said your pets could size me up."

"I said *a* pet could size up *a* human."

"Hypothetically, you mean?"

"Yeah."

"Not necessarily *this* human."

"No, not you."

"Then why, exactly, did you bring this up?"

"I was just thinking—you and I obviously suffered from bad judgment when we hooked up with our former spouses, Unhappily. Maybe we should have dogs or cats or whatever," he suggested.

"You mean we need to be looked after," she responded.

"For lack of a better way to put it, yes."

"I suppose I can't argue with that."

"I know someone who brings all of his dates home to meet his Russian wolfhound, Boris."

"Boris? As in Yeltsin?" Laura asked.

"No—as in Badenov. He never outgrew Rocky and Bullwinkle!" he explained.

"You have an interesting bunch of friends for a small-town boy, Misery."

"You said you grew up in a small town."

"I did."

"Then you should know that the real oddballs live in small towns."

"If you don't count the serial killers and mass murderers."

"They're not odd, just sick."

"True."

"What was your small town like?"

"Warm, friendly, homey, comfortable—but not terribly exciting," she remembered.

"My ex-wife would have said 'boring,'" he typed.

"I never thought of my hometown as boring. It wasn't the most exciting place on Earth, but I liked it the way it was," she told him.

"I feel the same way. That's why I never left, why I still live here."

"I left. Do you think I'm wrong to have done so?" she asked.

"A lot of people leave small towns to go to big cities."

"That's not what I asked."

"I know. I have to tell you, I'm not the most objective guy you could find on this particular issue, since my ex-wife's desire to escape was a major factor in the breakup of our marriage."

"Then you'd say I was wrong to leave?"

"I'd say that's your business."

But the truth was, Ben had *very* strong feelings on that topic.

Are all men alike? Laura wondered.

Misery had been careful not to judge her openly—his answer to her question was probably the most diplomatic she'd ever heard—but she could tell he had strong negative feelings about that sort of thing. Maybe all men felt that way. Maybe women were only deluding themselves, thinking men were ready to accept women who wanted careers *and* marriage. Maybe no man could accept her ambitions.

What do you expect? The man's been burned in the worst kind of way.

Ben wouldn't have been so kind. In fact, he hadn't been. In the end, he'd been downright nasty. Unforgiving. Unyielding. The day Laura left Fowler Falls, he'd made her feel as though she were the lowest form of life on Earth. Maybe even lower than that. If such a thing were possible.

He made me feel like a traitor, she recalled. *Un-American.*

Misery, however, was different. No matter how he felt, he didn't try to force his attitudes on her. He kept his negative feelings to himself. He respected her attitudes and needs.

At least he does now.

She wondered if his position would be the same if they were involved, if they were engaged in an intimate relationship. He and his wife certainly hadn't seen eye to eye on it. She and Ben hadn't, that was for sure.

You're just being paranoid, she told herself. *Not all men are like Ben.*

She had Ben on the brain. Probably because she knew she was going to be seeing him over the weekend, she decided as she finished packing her bag. She wasn't looking forward to it. *Just when the wounds were starting to heal, I go home and Ben rubs salt in them,* she thought miserably.

She packed some casual clothes, knowing she would have no need for anything dressy. It was going to be an informal weekend, as her weekends in Fowler Falls always were. *It's an informal town,* she thought. *No one to impress.*

Not even my ex-husband.

4

Laura knew she was getting close. The last house she'd passed was four miles back. That would have been the Adams farm, and there weren't any closer to town. Fowler Falls was little more than a handful of families and a dozen or so shops and businesses all clustered together in the middle of nowhere. Her mother called it picturesque. Her father used to say if you blinked while driving through town, you would pass through the town without ever seeing it. It wasn't far from the truth.

They were both right, Laura thought wryly as she passed the white roadside sign reading, Welcome To Fowler Falls, Pop. 342. People waved to her as she drove through town en route to Nick's home. Most of them had known her since she was a child. All of them were familiar faces. Too familiar at times, she decided now. Reminders of a life she wished to forget.

Laura smiled to herself as she approached the Roadside Café. Someone had altered the large painted sign on the side of the brick building facing the small parking lot. It now read Roadkill Café.

Much more appropriate, Laura thought, remembering what the cuisine at Ned Walters's establishment had been like. It brought a grimace to her face, as always. She didn't doubt that a lot of the townspeople believed he really *did* serve roadkill.

She tried to look as if she couldn't care less when she passed Ben's shop. *Look, but don't let them know that you're looking,* she told herself as she watched Sam and Ray work on a pickup truck out on the lot. She didn't see Ben. He was probably inside—in the garage or in the office. She hoped he was, anyway. She hoped she wouldn't have to see him on this trip. It would be so much easier—so much more bearable—if she didn't. Was it too much to hope for?

Maybe he went fishing, Laura thought. *He used to love fishing—most likely still does.* If she was lucky, he'd gone fishing for the entire weekend.

When the shop wasn't busy, when they were all caught up and had nothing pending, he, Sam and Ray used to close up and head off to their favorite fishing hole. She used to accuse them of hoping business would be slow. Actually, Sam and Ray *did*. She'd never been quite sure about Ben.

There were some good memories, weren't there? she asked herself as she turned the corner, catching sight of her brother's house as the auto body shop disappeared from sight. She breathed an inward sigh of relief. One hurdle cleared.

In all those years—there had to be.

As she braked to a stop in the driveway in front of the Harper house, three of her brother's four children scampered across the yard to greet her. Nick, Jr., the oldest, was the spitting image of his father, with his unruly dark hair and dark eyes; petite, blond Katie looked a great deal like her mother; little Gwen, now three, didn't look like either of them but got her coloring from generations of copper-haired, green-eyed Harpers. She was going to be a knockout, Laura decided, while Katie would be classically pretty. Nick would be constantly chasing girls away.

"Aunt Laura!" A shout came from seven-year-old Nick. It seemed like only yesterday he'd been a newborn baby, coming home from the hospital for the first time.

"Hi, Aunt Laura!" chirped Katie, who was now five.

"Hiii!" This was Gwen.

Laura hugged both Nicky and Katie as she got out of the car, then scooped Gwen up in her arms and carried her across the yard, en route to the house. She did love children, and she adored Nick's kids. She did want children of her own though. "You have grown—all of you," she told them. "Has it been that long since the last time I was here?"

"It's been a long time," Nicky told her. She realized then that she'd been avoiding her hometown for far too long. She'd let her problems—hers and Ben's—take precedence over everything else.

"Did you bring us anything?" Katie wanted to know. Even as she asked, the child was eagerly searching Laura's pockets. Nicky quickly joined in, giggling mischievously.

"Of course," Laura told her. "Would I come without gifts?" The children knew only too well that she wouldn't. She never did.

Her sister-in-law, Nick's wife, Sherry, emerged from the house as Laura started up the front steps. "I thought it had to be you—they don't even get that excited when their father comes home," Sherry said, gesturing to Laura to come on into the house. She held the door, stepping aside as Laura entered, leaving the children to play in the yard.

"It's nice to have such a warm greeting," Laura admitted. "When I come home to my apartment in Chicago, there's no one there to meet me." That was, she'd often thought, the loneliest feeling in the world.

"Maybe you should get a cat," Sherry suggested. She'd hesitated momentarily, as if wanting to make another suggestion but not daring to do so.

Laura shook her head. "My building doesn't allow pets." She'd considered that one herself; she'd been willing to consider just about anything.

"A bird, then. Birds and fish are usually allowed even where dogs and cats aren't. It's companionship, even if it's not of the human variety."

"I could always get a mynah bird and call it Ben," Laura said lightly. "You know it's funny—I had a conversation with someone else on this same topic just last night." A bird might not be such a bad idea. At least it could talk, even if it couldn't really carry on a conversation.

"Getting a pet?"

"Something like that, yes," Laura said with a nod. "Someone was telling me what a good judge of people animals are." She wanted to tell Sherry about Misery Loves Company, but wasn't sure it was the right time. What could she tell, anyway? What did she know herself?

"Someone?" Sherry asked with a sly smile. "Would that by any chance be a *male* someone?" So much for waiting for the right time. The door had already been opened.

"Yes, but before you go jumping to the wrong conclusions, it's not *that* kind of relationship," Laura told her. "This is someone I met on a computer network." She was careful to make their association seem as casual as possible. She didn't want to invite any questions she wouldn't be able to answer.

Sherry was still smiling. "Stranger things *have* happened."

"Laura's in town."

Ben looked up from the auto body he was working on as Ray entered the garage. "Where'd you hear that?" he wanted to know. He assumed it had come from the town rumor mill, which wasn't entirely reliable.

"Didn't hear it anywhere," Ray told him. "I saw her. Just now."

"Where?" Ben suddenly stood up, showing an interest he hadn't felt before.

"Driving down Main Street. She came right by here not two minutes ago," Ray told him. He gestured toward the large doors leading out to the town's main drag, showing the route Laura had taken.

"Did she see you?" Ben asked. Maybe he could get by with pretending not to know she was in town.

"I don't think she even looked this way," Ray said, shaking his head. He seemed surprised by her lack of interest.

"Right. Why would she?" Ben would never have admitted it, not even to his brothers, but he was deeply disappointed that Laura had not even looked his way. *She really doesn't care,* he thought miserably. He wished he didn't care so much. He wished it didn't matter to him whether she was here or not—whether she'd looked his way or not.

"She was probably heading for Nick's." Ray stated the obvious conclusion, since there was no one else in town she was likely to be visiting.

"What?" Ben asked, not having been paying attention. His thoughts were on his own feelings, his own pain and disappointment.

"She was probably headed for Nick's," Ray repeated.

"Oh, right."

"The Harpers are having some kind of big family thing this weekend," Ray offered as an explanation for her appearance in Fowler Falls. His tone, his expression seemed almost apologetic, and Ben hated that.

"Yeah," Ben said with a nod. "She'd have to have some special reason for being here."

"Huh?"

"She didn't want to live here," Ben told him. "She wasn't happy here. There would have to be something special going on for her being here now." She certainly wasn't here to see him. That much he knew.

Ray's body language made it obvious he didn't know what to say. He lingered only for a few moments before retreating to the nearest exit, ending the seemingly long, uncomfortable silence between them.

So...Laura's in town, Ben thought as he went back to work—or attempted to, anyway. No matter how hard he tried, he found it impossible to keep his mind on the task at hand. *No doubt for the weekend. She wouldn't be able to stand it any longer than that.*

Laura had made it painfully clear to him that she wasn't happy in Fowler Falls and never could be. She wasn't happy with *him*. She needed the bright lights, the energy, the nonstop excitement of a city like Chicago. She needed the powerful, successful men. She needed the challenges, she'd told him, the opportunities she'd never have in their peaceful little hometown. Needed them more than anything he could give her.

She needed to fulfill her ambitions. Without him.

With a vengeance Ben sanded the side of the car he'd been working on. He wasn't thinking about the car, though.

He was still thinking about Laura.

"I can't get over how much he's grown," Laura told Sherry as she bounced the youngest Harper child, ten-month-old Mickey, on her knee.

"They grow fast at Mickey's age," Sherry said with a nod, affectionately rumpling the boy's hair as they talked. "Sometimes I think he's growing too fast."

"You're so lucky," Laura told her. And she meant it. Ben didn't believe it, but she did want kids of her own.

Sherry eyed her suspiciously. "Don't tell me your biological clock is ticking," she exclaimed.

"You think I'm immune?" Laura wanted to know. Did everyone see her as a cold-blooded, unfeeling creature concerned only with career goals?

"No, it's not that," Sherry began, slightly embarrassed. "It's just that you've never seemed all that interested in having children of your own."

"You mean because of my career," Laura concluded. She was right. They did see her as less than human. Less than female. That hurt—more than she would ever admit.

"Well, yes."

"I'd like to think I could have both," Laura said. It was the truth. She'd always believed she *could* have both.

"But not with Ben." Sherry reached the same conclusion everyone else in Fowler Falls undoubtedly had.

"Ben didn't give me a choice. He gave me an ultimatum," she said gravely. He'd forced her to choose between him and her career—then had taken that decision out of her hands by filing for divorce.

"He didn't like you being away so much," Sherry told her. Laura should have expected that. Sherry had always liked Ben and hoped they would get back together.

Still, Laura couldn't hide her surprise that Sherry would be so blunt. "Hey, whose side are you on?" she asked, feigning anger at her sister-in-law.

"Yours," Sherry said quickly. "I know you still love him—"

"I'll get over him." Laura spoke with a finality she wasn't sure she really felt.

"Let me finish. I know you care about him, and the whole town knows he's still hung up on you," Sherry said. "We've always hoped that one day you'd get back together."

"'We'—as in you and Nick?" Laura asked. Laura already knew the answer to that but pushed Sherry to say the words anyway.

"No. 'We,' as in the entire population of Fowler Falls," Sherry told her.

Laura wrinkled her nose with disdain. If they only knew... "I doubt that."

"Don't. It's the truth."

Laura didn't doubt that for a moment. "With so many people rooting for us, how did we go so wrong?" Laura asked, querying herself more than Sherry. It was a question she'd posed to herself many times in the past.

"I've always thought it was a communications failure," Sherry offered as a possible explanation. It was a classic understatement if ever there was one.

"If you ask me, we communicated a little too much," Laura said in a slightly cynical tone. "Especially at the end." Trouble was, the communicating they had done was mostly of the high-decibel, total-lack-of-reason variety.

"I'm not talking about fighting," Sherry said quickly. "I'm talking about real, open, unmasked discussions. Being completely up-front about your feelings, your needs." They'd done that, Laura recalled. They just hadn't *listened* to each other.

Laura frowned. "I used to think there wasn't anything Ben and I didn't know about each other. We'd known each other so long, it was as if there was no mystery in our relationship. We actually could finish each other's sentences." *Maybe,* she thought now, *there was actually more mystery than could be considered safe for any couple.*

"But?"

"But at the end, I started to feel as though I didn't really know him at all—and he didn't really know me," Laura admitted. Actually, they'd been like total strangers at the end, she remembered.

"You probably didn't."

"Whaaat?" After hearing everyone, literally everyone, in Fowler Falls talk about how they were meant for each other, Sherry caught her off guard.

"I've always suspected that even though the two of you grew up together, each of you still saw the other as you were when you were kids in high school."

"I can't deny that," Laura said with a nod. "I thought he'd always be the dreamer he was back then, and he certainly never adjusted to the changes in me."

"I didn't think so," Sherry said, taking Mickey, whose nap time was fast approaching. She carried the child off to his room to put him down for a nap, leaving Laura alone with her thoughts.

Laura debated telling Sherry anything more about Misery Loves Company.

"I'll have a cheeseburger and fries, Marilyn," Ben told the waitress at the Roadside Café as he seated himself on a red vinyl stool at the lunch counter. "And make it to go." The café hadn't changed at all in forty years—except for the waitresses. Not the tables, not the red vinyl, not even the menu. Ned had gone from brown hair to gray, but that was about it.

"Busy today, huh?" Marilyn was a full-figured, overdone blonde who always looked as if she were about to bust out of her uniform.

Ben nodded. "Got one I have to have finished by two this afternoon, so I'll have to eat while I work," he told her.

"Can't Sam and Ray handle it?" the waitress asked. She'd offered more than once to help Ben make good use of his free time, but he'd always politely declined.

He shook his head. "For once, they're busy themselves."

"They didn't go fishing?" Marilyn didn't hide her surprise. Sam and Ray Westin were notorious goof-offs. Everyone in Fowler Falls knew it.

"Nope. I read the riot act to them about that." He checked out the doughnuts on display. "I'll take one of those long Johns, too. Chocolate." *So far, so good,* he thought. *She hasn't mentioned Laura. Maybe Laura hasn't been here yet.*

"Coming right up." She went for the doughnut case. "I hear your ex is in town."

He nodded. His luck had just run out. "So I've been told."

"You haven't seen her?" Marilyn seemed honestly surprised.

As will everyone else in town, he thought dismally. "Nope. No reason I should." Laura certainly didn't want to see him.

"I don't know...Fowler Falls *is* a small town," she reminded him.

"Too small for the two of us," Ben acknowledged. Obviously. That was why she so seldom came to town. She didn't want to run into him.

"You're bound to run into her sooner or later."

"Not if I can help it." He meant it. The last thing he needed—or wanted—was to run into Laura. But could they successfully avoid each other?

A strange look suddenly came over Marilyn's face. "Well, I'll be—look who just walked in," she said slowly, nodding toward the front door as if whoever had just entered were armed and dangerous.

"Who?" Ben shifted on his stool to get a look—and saw Laura coming toward him. Much as he hated to admit it, she looked beautiful with her hair long and loose, wearing a soft, sapphire-blue jumpsuit. She also looked out of place.

When she saw him, she stopped in her tracks, drawing in a deep breath. "Hello, Ben," she said finally.

"Laura," he responded with a nod. *Go home, Laura,* he was thinking.

"How have you been?" Her voice was strained. She was clearly *not* happy to see him.

His jaw tightened. "Do you really care, or are you just trying to be polite?" he asked. Mentally he reprimanded himself for that. He didn't want her to see how much he was still hurting.

"Don't start, Ben," she said wearily.

He turned back to the waitress. "How long on that cheeseburger, Marilyn?" he asked irritably. He wanted to get his order and get out of there as quickly as possible.

"A couple of minutes at least." Marilyn gave him an apologetic look.

He shot her a murderous look.

She shrugged. "Sorry."

"I don't suppose you'd consider delivering?" His voice was tight, irritated. He tried to hide his feelings, but to no avail.

Marilyn made a face. "Ned hire a delivery boy? He wouldn't hire waitresses if he didn't have to have somebody to wait tables."

Ben snorted, muttering something under his breath as he turned back to Laura. "Death in the family?" he wanted to know.

His tone was cold, unfriendly. Only if he'd said the words *go home* could the message have been any clearer.

"No. Why do you ask?"

"I figure it would take a funeral or something like that to get you here," he said. "I don't recall you coming around here just because you want to."

"If I'd known I'd run into you, I *wouldn't* have come!" she shot back at him.

"Don't worry. You won't be running into me again." He pushed past her and stormed out of the restaurant with Marilyn running after him, doggie bag in hand.

"We can't even be civil to each other," Laura told Nick and Sherry over dinner that night. The meal was as down-home as Sherry could make it: fried chicken, potatoes, baked beans, hot biscuits and homemade blueberry pie.

"What did he say to you?" her brother asked, passing the beans to his son.

"He wanted to know who died."

"*What?*" Nick accepted the plate of biscuits his wife passed across the table to him.

"He asked if someone in the family had died," Laura said again. "He said he couldn't imagine that I'd be here unless I had to be."

"He's bitter, Laura," Sherry insisted. "He still loves you."

"He has a funny way of showing it," Laura said, not bothering to conceal her annoyance. "He did everything but point me toward the highway and tell me to go back to Chicago."

"He does, believe me."

"I find it hard to believe he feels anything but contempt for me."

Laura didn't say so, but she wished she'd stayed in Chicago.

5

———→ ◄———

Think, Westin.

Ben stared at the blank computer screen for a long moment, debating within himself before deciding against telling Unhappily Unwed about his unpleasant encounter with Laura over the weekend. *Don't want to sound like a whiner,* he told himself. Besides, they'd talked about their exes enough. Was this any way to get to know each other?

"How was your weekend?" he typed. *Mine was the pits,* he thought.

"Uneventful. I went to a family reunion back home."

"You must have a normal family if you can describe it as uneventful. I know of reunions where the police had to be called." *Namely mine.*

"Sounds like fun."

"It is if you like lineups and handcuffs." *She thinks I'm kidding.*

"I like your sense of humor, Misery."

"You think I'm joking?" *Keep her going, Westin.*

"Oh, come on, Misery."

"I'm serious, Unhappily," he assured her. *Really I am.*

"You have a wonderful sense of humor."

"Well, thank you—I think!"

"Ever consider leaving that small town of yours, Misery?"

"Never." *Laura wanted me to.*

"Never? Never even *thought* about it?" she asked.

"Nope. Everything I could ever want or need is right here." *Laura never understood that.*

"Unique," she decided.

"Why do you say that?" *Laura would have said "foolish."*

"Most people want something more, no matter what they already have."

Ben hesitated. There *was* one thing he wanted that he didn't have, that he no longer had, but...

"Not me," he typed. It was the truth.

"I always did. I suppose I should have been satisfied—I had a good life—but I wasn't. No matter how good I had it, I always wanted more."

Sounds like Laura, Ben thought but didn't openly express the sentiment. "I guess that's just human nature," he responded. *For some humans, anyway.*

"You mean like eating, breathing and sleeping?"

"Something like that, yeah." *It was for Laura.*

"It's a relief to communicate with someone who doesn't think I'm some kind of monster for having ambitions."

Laura would never believe this, Ben thought as he typed his response. "Nothing wrong with wanting to better one's self." *Unless it was at the expense of one's marriage.*

"That's what I tried to tell my ex-husband, but he wasn't having any of it."

"Maybe he felt like he was competing with your career for your attention." *That's how I felt.*

"Is that how you felt, Misery?"

"I beg your pardon?" *Is this woman clairvoyant, or what?*

"Is that how your ex-wife made you feel—like you had to compete with her career for her attentions?"

"Most of the time, yes." *Just about all the time, actually.*

"My ex didn't think there was any competition. He thought I only cared about my career, which couldn't have been farther from the truth."

"Mine really did feel that way." *That was the truth.*

"Huh?"

"Her career came first—and last. She only went through the motions of being a wife." *At the end, not even that.*

"I tried to be a good wife. It was a juggling act, I admit, but I tried. It just wasn't enough for my husband—ex-husband."

"Some guys are never satisfied." *I would have been.*

"He wasn't."

"I didn't mind my wife having a career, as long as it didn't take all of her time." *And all of her attention.*

"But it did?"

"Did it! If we'd had thirty-hour days, there still wouldn't have been any real quality time for us." *A little ambition goes a long way.*

"That bad?"

"That bad." *Worse, if you want the truth.*

"I used to feel guilty about spending so much time away from home, away from my husband—but hindsight being twenty-twenty, I think I probably didn't really have anything to feel guilty about."

"Oh?" *Was she saying the marriage would have failed anyway?*

"I doubt that anything I could have done—short of giving up my career entirely—would have made him happy."

"I know that feeling of hopelessness. I always wondered what it was that I didn't do but should have done to make her happy."

"I came to the conclusion that *I* just wasn't enough to make my ex happy—no matter what I did or didn't do."

"Maybe I was in the same boat." *Sure felt like it.*

"I suspect you probably were."

"Hard to believe, isn't it?" *What were the odds, anyway?*

"That we're in the same boat?"

"No. That we both married people we'd known all our lives, but didn't really know them at all."

"Do we ever really know anyone?"

"One of life's great mysteries, I'm sure." *No doubt about it.*

Laura was beginning to feel as if she *did* know Misery Loves Company. At least she knew him as well as she wanted to know any man right now, which meant keeping him at arm's length—at least for now.

Zara was right, she decided. *This is really a wonderful way to get to know another person. No distractions such as concerns with physical appearances— one's own or the other person's—to get in the way.*

Misery and I, we're sort of like electronic soul mates.

She was still toying with the idea of suggesting that they meet face-to-face, but continued to wonder if it still wasn't too soon.

Could ruin everything, she told herself. *What if there's no chemistry?*

"Off in the clouds again, I see."

Laura looked up to see Zara standing on the other side of the desk, regarding her with a wicked grin. "I beg your pardon?"

"You looked a million miles away," Zara told her.

"I took your advice."

"Which advice is that?"

"The computer network. I tried it."

"Oh, yeah?" Suddenly Laura had Zara's undivided attention.

"It was... interesting."

"You met someone," Zara guessed.

"I didn't say that."

"You didn't have to."

"So, what makes you think I met anyone special?" Laura wanted to know.

"The look on your face," Zara said with a sly smile.

"Which is?"

"Suggestive, to say the least."

"That bad?"

"No, that *good*," Zara told her. "So, tell me—who is he and what's he like?"

"I don't really know who he is."

"Huh?"

"You know how everybody uses those funny little names... well, we've never told each other our real names," Laura admitted.

"So you know him as—"

"Misery Loves Company."

"Original. Very original."

"And I'm Unhappily Unwed," Laura told her.

"Takes guts to advertise it," she responded.

"Thanks."

"So... what *do* you know about this guy?"

"That he went through a messy divorce, too."

Zara winced. "Two bruised and battered egos. Great," she groaned.

"Zara—"

"Do you by chance know anything else about him?"

"Well, so far it seems that we share a lot of the same attitudes and some common interests," Laura told her.

"At least that's a good start," Zara acknowledged with a nod.

"I thought so."

"You're interested."

"Well, yes."

"You'd like to meet him? Face-to-face, I mean."

"I suppose so."

Zara shot her a disbelieving look. "You suppose so?"

"Yes. Yes, I would," Laura said, nodding.

"Then why don't you?"

"I think it may be a little too soon," Laura replied, worrying aloud.

"By whose standards?"

"Mine," Laura said. "I still don't feel like I know him well enough."

"Talk about cautious!" Zara laughed, shaking her head. "You should be heading the loan department."

Laura was still thinking about it long after Zara had retreated to the outer office. She still had mixed feelings about this relationship, such as it was. There hadn't been anyone since Ben. She hadn't *wanted* anyone since Ben.

Now, she wasn't sure *what* she wanted.

* * *

"Who is she?"

Ben looked up from the auto body he was sanding. "Beg your pardon?" he asked, not sure he understood.

"Who is she?" Sam repeated the question.

"Who is who?" Ben really didn't know what he was talking about.

"The new lady in your life."

"You're making even less sense than usual," Ben told him. "Would you care to elaborate?"

"Come *on,* big brother—we all know there's somebody new in your life," Sam persisted. "We also know it's *not* somebody from around here." It was only too clear to Ben that his brother was not about to back off without an explanation.

"We all? We who?"

"Well, Ray and me."

"That figures."

"Who *is* she?" Sam asked again.

Ben got to his feet. "First of all, little brother, you're way off base," he told Sam. "There's no new lady in my life." He wiped the grease from his hands onto the dirty, dark blue mechanic's overalls he wore.

"Ray said you'd say that."

"I'm saying it because there *is* no lady," he said firmly. "I've met somebody, yeah, but there's no romance. She's more like a pen pal."

"A what?"

"A pen pal. An electronic pen pal," Ben told him.

"Sounds weird."

"Yeah, I guess it does."

"How'd you meet her?" Sam wanted to know.

"The computer I use in the office," Ben said, wiping the back of his hand across his brow. "The new software I bought enables me to communicate with others with personal computers via networks and electronic bulletin boards. I met this lady on a network of divorce survivors."

"What's her name?"

"I don't know."

Sam gave him a quizzical look.

"Nobody on those networks uses real names," Ben explained. "They use handles that say something about who they are—like the people who write to 'Dear Abby.'"

"Like 'Sleepless in Seattle,'" Sam said.

"Exactly."

"So where's she from?"

Ben hesitated. "I don't know that, either," he admitted.

Sam couldn't hide his surprise. "What *do* you know about her?" he asked, beginning to wonder.

"That I like her. That we understand each other."

Sam nodded. "Good start."

"I'm glad you approve," Ben responded with mild amusement in his voice.

"Are you ever planning to meet her?" Sam asked. "I mean *really* meet her?"

"I don't know. Maybe."

"You should."

"Oh? And why is that?" Ben asked.

"You're still hurting over Laura." Ben started to shake his head, but Sam stopped him. "Don't try to deny it, big brother. Everybody knows it. A new woman in your life is exactly what you need."

"Thank you, Dr. Freud." Ben chuckled with a dismissive wave of his hand, indicating that it was time for Sam to get his butt back to work.

But Ben was thinking: *If only it was so easy.*

"My family thinks I should remarry," Laura confided. "Or at the very least, get a new man in my life." *As if it's all that easy.*

"Mine, too."

"Your family thinks you should have a new man in your life?" *Sorry, I couldn't resist that one.*

"Very funny."

"It's been that kind of day." *It's been that kind of week.*

"That bad, eh?"

"Worse." *Much worse.*

"Sorry to hear it."

"Thanks." *I wonder if he really means it.*

"My well-meaning relatives think all I have to do is go out and meet somebody and everything will magically be all right."

"Sounds familiar."

"You get the same song and dance?"

"I think they must all be using the same sheet music." *Either that, or we're related.*

"But only someone who's been there can really understand what it's like for us."

"That's true." *Truer words were never spoken.*

"I guess that's why the bulletin board where we met was so popular."

"No doubt." *A lot of us in the same boat.*

"We survivors of the divorce wars have to stick together."

"You can say that again," Laura typed.

"We survivors of the—"

"Don't take me literally, Misery. I was only kidding." *So is he, obviously.*

"Just wanted to see if you were paying attention."

"Right."

"Do you like movies, Unhappily?"

The question took Laura by surprise. "I love movies—but why do you ask?"

"I was at the video store last night."

"Let me guess—the local video store's in a building that used to be someone's house or garage, right?"

"Right—but how did you know?"

"I told you. I grew up in a small town. It's fairly typical." *Small towns have that in common.*

"Oh."

"Well, which is it, Misery?"

"What do you mean?"

"The video store—a house or a garage?"

"Garage."

"Just like in my hometown."

"Yeah?"

"Would I lie to you?"

"I don't know. Would you?"

Laura frowned. He wasn't sure. But then, she should be able to understand that, she told herself. After all, she'd been there, too. "No, I wouldn't lie to you, Misery."

"Thanks."

"Do you believe me?"

"Yes."

"Thank *you*. Now, where were we?"

"I asked if you liked movies."

"And I told you I did."

"What kind do you prefer?"

"Comedies, mostly. Especially good romantic comedies."

"Old movies?"

Laura smiled, recalling one in particular she'd loved, a 1947 musical comedy called *Down to Earth.* "Some. What about you?"

"I like action. Adventure," he answered.

"Macho stuff." *Ben liked "macho stuff."*

"Well—yeah."

"Why am I not surprised?" she asked.

"Hey, now, am I being put down here?"

"Not at all," Laura assured him. "I was simply making an observation."

"Which is?"

"That women like a variety of movies, while men's tastes tend to be considerably narrower."

"That's not true! I like different kinds of movies!"

"Really."

"One of these days, I'll prove it," he promised.

"And just how will you do that?"

"We'll go to the movies."

"Together?"

"Well, yes—that's the general idea."

Laura smiled. It was *his* suggestion. He wanted to meet her.

6

⟶ ⟵

"What kind of music do you like, Misery?" Laura wanted to know.

"Country." *Ben liked country music.*

"Just country?"

"Is there any other kind?"

Ben felt exactly the same way. "Well, yes. There's pop and rock and jazz and opera."

"Opera? Puhlllease!"

He sounded so typically male.

"Who are your favorites?"

"Let me see...Clint Black, Trisha Yearwood, Vince Gill. But my all-time favorite is Dakota Law."

"Dakota Law? He's my ex-husband's favorite, too."

"I'm not surprised. He's got a huge following."

Men must favor country, she concluded. "So I hear."

"What about you?"

Not country, that's for sure. "I like variety. Mostly rock—especially Chelsea Stone," she told him.

"Chelsea Stone? She crossed over, you know."

"I know. Teamed up with your Dakota Law, I hear."

"Yeah, she did," he recalled.

"I only discovered her recently—I listen to her old stuff all the time now," she explained.

She loved Chelsea Stone's early recordings. "The stuff she did with Tucker Gable?"

"Tucker Gable. Without a doubt, one of the sexiest men in music." *One of the sexiest men anywhere on the planet.*

"If you happen to like the type."

"What woman wouldn't?" She couldn't even imagine *that!*

"I can think of a few."

"I can't." *Truthfully.*

"Is this turning into a debate, or what?"

"Could be, Misery."

Sure sounds like it from where I am sitting. "Is this a healthy sign?" he asked.

"Of what?" She wasn't sure she understood.

"Of us!" he responded.

"How so?" What was he getting at? she wondered.

"It would seem that we're able to disagree without ruining our relationship."

Relationship? "Well, ours isn't exactly a typical relationship. And I can't say I've ever heard of a couple parting ways over a difference of opinion over music.'' At least that was one thing that *hadn't* come between her and Ben.

''Yeah, I guess you're right.... I wonder what else we disagree on.''

Do we really want to know? She wasn't sure. ''Probably a lot of things.''

''You're probably right.'' *But will we ever know for sure?*

''I probably am. What about books?'' she asked. *Did he like to read at all? Ben wasn't much of a reader.*

''What about them?''

''Do you read?'' *That must have sounded snotty.*

''Sometimes,'' he replied.

''What do you prefer?'' she wanted to know.

''*TV Guide* or *Playboy*,'' he answered.

''*Playboy?*'' *I should have expected that.*

''I guess that one doesn't count, really. I just look at the pictures,'' he told her.

''Funny, Misery.''

''I thought so.''

A warped sense of humor, too. Charming. ''I'll just bet you did.''

''So what do you like to read?'' he asked.

''Novels, mostly. Sidney Sheldon, Judith Krantz, Jackie Collins.''

''You like big commercial fiction, then,'' he concluded.

She nodded to herself. He knew them even if he didn't read them. ''Not all of it. There are a lot of books on the bestseller lists that wouldn't be there if it were left up to me.''

''Major meow!''

''What?'' *Maybe I should have given him a smart-alecky answer, after all.*

''Major meow—as in catty remark!''

Catty? This came as a surprise. ''Funny.''

''Very.''

Much as she hated to, she would have to sign off. ''Got to sign off now, Misery,'' she typed. ''It's almost midnight.''

''That's not late.''

By whose estimation? Laura wondered. ''It is when I have an early appointment in the morning.''

''You know what they say about all work and no play.''

Only too well. ''I know all play won't pay the bills.''

''Party pooper.''

Where had she heard *that* before? ''There's always tomorrow, Misery.''

''Same time, same place?''

''As always.''

As Laura shut down her computer, she thought about Misery. Obviously he enjoyed their late-night on-line conversations as much as she did. A nameless, faceless man on a computer with a quick wit beat a long, lonely night with no one any day of the week.

Could a face-to-face meeting be far off?

* * *

Ben was thinking exactly the same thing.

He'd been thinking about it for some time now, actually. Wondering what she looked like, where she lived, what she did for a living. Wondering how he would be spending his evenings now if it weren't for their on-line chance meeting.

What's her name? he wondered. *Amy? Abby? Brittany? Charlotte? Jill? Susan?*

There was so much he didn't yet know about her. So much he wanted to know. Nothing like a woman of mystery to pique the curiosity of a man who'd been alone longer than he wanted to be.

How long has it been? he asked himself now. How long had it been since he'd cared enough about a woman to be curious? How long since he'd felt enough interest in a woman to warrant even a second look?

Not since Laura.

Not before, and not since. He hadn't allowed himself to care, or even to feel a mild degree of interest in a woman. He had no desire to be burned again.

But now . . . maybe the healing process had finally begun. Maybe he was finally getting over her. Hopefully he was getting over her. He didn't enjoy pain— physical or emotional.

At the moment, he wasn't sure how he felt about that.

Sam would say he didn't *want* to get over her, that it was easier to just go on as he was, mourning the loss of the only woman he'd ever loved and using his grief as an excuse to go on feeling sorry for himself rather than put it behind him and move on. But Sam would be wrong. This wasn't easier than anything—except perhaps death.

He hadn't wanted to meet anyone new because a new relationship required a degree of risk he hadn't been willing to take. A degree of risk he'd never *had* to take because he'd never even dated anyone other than Laura. There had never been anyone for him but the girl next door, the woman he'd grown up with. That had been enough. More than enough.

He'd never had to deal with the pain of rejection. He'd never had to worry about how a woman might react when he asked her out or whether she would be willing to see him again if they did have a first date.

At least not until his marriage broke up.

Laura wondered—again—what her computer friend looked like.

Tall, dark, classically handsome? Short, fair, bookish? Fair or swarthy? Intellectual or athletic? Macho or Mr. Sensitive? Laura knew she wouldn't stop wondering until she met him.

She'd tried to conjure up an image of him in her mind, a mental portrait of what he might look like. What she wanted him to look like, actually. *Tall, dark, athletic, with a quick wit and a wonderful smile. Probably named Josh or Dan,* she thought. *Macho but not too macho. Probably drives a Jeep.*

Oddly enough, that mental picture bore a strong resemblance to her ex-husband.

That should be the last thing I want, she told herself.

Why haven't I learned my lesson—yet?

The answer, she decided, was actually quite simple. She fell in love with and married Ben because she was attracted to that type of man, so why wouldn't she find other men like him attractive?

Because our marriage was an unqualified disaster, because loving him brought me so much pain, she thought miserably. *I should be repulsed by men like him.*

But she wasn't.

"Where would you go—if you could go anywhere in the world you wanted?" *Let's see how she answers that one,* Ben thought.

"Is this a trick question?" Laura typed.

"No. I really want to know." He really did.

"All right. I'd go to the Italian Riviera."

Laura had wanted to go to Italy. "Why?" *Were her reasons the same as Laura's?*

"Why?"

"Yeah, why? Why not the French Riviera? Why not Rome or Paris?" *Why Italy?*

"Excuse me?"

"What makes the Italian Riviera so special?" he asked. *Why did it bother him?*

"I don't know. I've heard things, I've read a lot about it. It just sounds so appealing—the resorts mingling with the small towns and fishing villages, the sandy beaches and the fields of roses and carnations, the almond, peach and apricot blossoms, the Mediterranean stretching as far as the eye can see."

She'd described it so well, he could almost see it. "Sounds like a little town I know not far from here."

"Where would you go?" she asked.

He didn't hesitate. He'd always known the answer. "Hawaii," he answered.

"You didn't even have to think about it?" she asked.

She seemed surprised. "Nope."

"Okay, I'll bite. Why Hawaii?"

Did she even have to ask? "Sandy beaches, the Pacific Ocean, suntanned girls—women—in thong bikinis." Thong bikinis. That brought a pleasurable sigh.

"That's what I call a deep appreciation of nature!"

"Oh, I definitely appreciate nature," he assured her. *In its rawest form.*

"I can tell."

"Looks like there's not much chance of us bumping into each other on vacation," he typed. *Kind of like Laura and me.*

"Probably not."

"Have you traveled much?" Laura always yearned to travel.

"Some. But not nearly as much as I'd like," she told him.

"Where have you been?"

"London—a couple of times. Amsterdam. That was a couple of months ago. And New York. I've been there four times, always on business. What about you?"

"Canada. Camping, hunting, fishing."

"That's it?"

"That's it. I was there for two weeks, right after the divorce. It's a beautiful country."

Ben paused for a moment, recalling that trip. Sam and Ray had gone to Canada every year, but Ben had always passed because the idea of "roughing it" in the Canadian wilderness hadn't appealed to Laura. She didn't want to go, and he didn't want to be away from her for two weeks, so he invariably denied himself his second fondest wish—and lost the first anyway.

He wondered how this woman felt about it?

He likes camping. Ben liked camping.

Laura frowned. She *didn't* like camping. She hated bugs and snakes and sleeping on the ground. She wasn't wild about cooking over an open fire and refused to clean fish. Since their marriage, Ben had stopped going on those camping trips with his brothers because of her, because she didn't want to go. She wondered if he resented her for that, if that was at least part of the reason he finally decided to end their marriage.

She had no idea why she felt guilty about that. She'd never stopped him from going. She'd never asked him not to go. She would never have asked him not to do anything he really wanted to do. Had he bothered to ask, she would have told him that. She would have told him she knew how much it meant to him; she would have told him it was all right.

She would never have made the kind of unreasonable demands on him that he'd made on her. She would have accepted those interests they didn't share. She wouldn't have held him back as he had her.

Is that why I'm holding back? she wondered now. *Is that why, as curious as I am about Misery, as much as I want to meet him, a part of me still refuses to take the relationship even one step further?*

She hadn't even told him her name. There had been times she'd wanted to—lots of times—but she hadn't. There was so much she hadn't told him—and, she suspected, so much he hadn't told her, as well.

Why?

He didn't even know where she lived. Was she really concerned only about safety, or was she just reluctant to let anyone—any man—get close to her? Were they, when all was said and done, just two people who'd been so deeply hurt that the only kind of relationship either of them could initiate was one that allowed them that necessary degree of distance?

How long, she wondered, *before I really put the past behind me and get on with my life?*

* * *

I want to meet her. I do. So why do I keep putting it off? What am I afraid of?

Ben had lost track of how many times he'd asked himself that question. He already knew the answer but still he kept asking the question.

It was simple. He didn't want to be hurt again.

Once was enough, thank you very much.

But did he want to spend the rest of his life alone?

No. He didn't even have to think about that one. He didn't want to be alone. He had never wanted to be alone. For as long as he could remember, he'd always seen himself as a family man, always pictured himself with a wife and children. Until last year, he'd believed the wife in that mental family portrait would be Laura. When they split, he thought that was the end of the dream. But now...now he wasn't so sure. He wasn't sure it really was the end of the dream, and he wasn't ready to give it up, at any rate. But he also wasn't sure he had the courage to pursue it.

Maybe he could have that life after all. Maybe he could have it with someone else. Maybe he could have it with Unhappily Unwed. Maybe he could still have that house with the white picket fence, the wife who was there at least part of the time and a couple of kids.

That's crazy, he told himself. *I've never even met her! I wouldn't know her if I bumped into her on the street. I don't know her name. I don't know where she lives.*

What he did know, however, was that she, too, had been badly burned by a failed relationship. She'd also lost someone, someone she'd loved all her life. She, too, had ended up with a divorce she never wanted. And like him, she was struggling to go on, to start a new life, to find happiness without the husband she'd obviously loved deeply.

And, he suspected, she also still harbored strong feelings for her former spouse. Not in spite of her love, but because of it.

Just as I do, Ben thought. *We have so much in common. We could turn to each other, help each other work through those feelings.*

And with luck, maybe we could even give each other something more.

"How do you feel about marriage?"

The question took Laura totally by surprise. "I beg your pardon?"

"I asked how you felt about marriage," he repeated.

Why is he asking? she wondered. "Right now? At this moment?"

"That'll do for starters," he told her.

Should I be truthful here? "It scares me."

"Scares you? Why?"

Shouldn't that be obvious? "I suppose because mine ended so badly. You've been there. Doesn't it scare you?" she asked.

"Sometimes."

"Only sometimes?" *It scares me all the time.*

"Yeah."

Not me. I don't want to be hurt again. "I'm not sure I understand."

"Well, there are times the thought of taking another stab at marriage—if you'll pardon the expression—scares the living daylights out of me."

My sentiments exactly. "That's how I feel."

"But there are other times . . ."

Other times? "Go on," she urged.

"There are other times when I remember the good times," he told her.

There were good times in your marriage? "Good times?" she asked. *I only remember pain.*

"Yeah. My ex and I did have some good times. Wonderful times, in fact," he recalled.

Good times.

Laura thought about it for a long moment before typing her response: "We did, too—my ex-husband and me, I mean. More good than bad, actually," she admitted. *If I'm going to be honest here.*

"Same here," he responded.

"I do miss those times." *I really do.*

"So do I."

"I suppose that's what makes it all so painful." It was hard to let go of the good times.

"I'm sure. Can't imagine anybody missing the bad stuff," he said. *I certainly didn't.*

"No, definitely not," she agreed. *But it's hard to forget the bad stuff.*

"It's thinking about those good times that makes me wish I had it all back, makes me wish I could have it again," he confided.

"With your ex?" She wasn't sure she wanted to hear the answer.

"Not necessarily."

"As long as we're being so open and honest here, I have to admit that I do understand how you feel." She really did.

"You've had those feelings yourself, haven't you?"

Did she really want to admit it? Laura hesitated. "Yes."

"It gets pretty lonely, doesn't it?"

"Lonely" didn't quite cover it. "It did."

"Did?"

Might as well be totally honest, she decided. "Until I met you—or whatever this is called."

" 'Meet' will do."

It certainly would, Laura thought, *if only I could get up the nerve.*

7

Ben had given this a great deal of thought.

"I could ask her to have dinner with me."

If I knew where she lived. If we're at least in the same state.

Kneeling beside the vehicle he was working on, Ben was talking to himself rather than to Sam and Ray, who were with him in the garage taking a break, but he didn't realize he'd spoken the words aloud until his brothers responded.

"Sounds like a good idea to me," said Ray.

"Maybe you could take in a movie, too," Sam suggested.

They looked at each other, nodding enthusiastically.

Flushing, Ben looked up, realizing for the first time that he'd been thinking aloud. He would have preferred not to respond at all, but it was too late for that now. "Yeah, maybe I will," he said distractedly. "She likes movies. That's a good idea."

I'll try just about anything at this point.

"What kind of movies does she like?" Ray popped open a can of soda. "Commercial or artsy-fartsy?" he wanted to know.

"Old movies."

"Maybe you'd better make it the video store, then, rather than the theater," Sam put in.

"Yeah," Ray agreed. "Rent a bunch of movies, call out for pizza, maybe make some popcorn."

"Cozy," Sam said with a nod, "but not all that romantic, if that's what you're trying for."

"That might seem too forward," Ben worried. "I can't very well say, 'Hey, let's have dinner, than go back to my place and watch some old movies.' Do you have any idea what that would sound like?"

Ray grinned.

"Like your intentions aren't strictly honorable?" Sam asked.

"Are they?" Ray asked.

They turned to each other again, grinning wickedly.

Ben shook his head, taking a deep breath. "The jury's still out on that one," he admitted.

It would help if I did know, actually.

"You don't know how you *feel* about her?" Ray asked, surprised. He passed Sam another can of soda.

"He's not sure about a lot of things," Sam put in.

"Nope," Ben said honestly. "I guess it's because we haven't met yet. I have feelings for her, yeah—but right now I'm not exactly sure what those feelings are." Admitting that made him feel like an idiot.

"Right," Ray droned.

"Makes sense," Sam said with a nod.

"No, it doesn't," Ben said, shaking his head, "but hopefully it will. Soon."

"You could ask him out, you know," Zara suggested. She sat on one corner of Laura's desk, her wild, bright curls seemingly set afire by sunlight streaming through the floor-to-ceiling windows.

"Have you ever *thought* about it?"

Laura, who looked and felt ultraconservative compared to her flamboyant assistant, shook her head. "I don't think so."

Definitely not my style.

Zara eyed her warily. "Don't tell me you're one of those old-fashioned women who waits for the man to make all the moves."

Laura gave her a tired smile. "I have no idea what kind of woman I am," she confessed.

"Come again?"

"When it comes to matters of the heart, I have no idea what my particular 'style' is," Laura told her, leaning back in her chair and smoothing the front of her yellow linen skirt. "After all, I was never really in circulation. I married my first love, the boy I grew up with. I never dated anyone else. I've never asked anyone out, and no one asked me out because they all knew I was with Ben." The admission made her realize what a traditional, small-town girl she really was.

A real bumpkin, now that I think about it.

"It's not all that hard, you know," Zara told her. "Asking a man out, I mean."

Laura gave a little laugh. "I'm sure you've done it many times." Zara was the type who definitely would not have trouble making the first move.

She probably does more often than not.

"I sure have," Zara said proudly.

"And with the greatest of ease, no doubt." She probably had some of the best pick-up lines ever heard by any member of the male species.

Not to mention totally original.

"Absolutely."

"I'm probably going to be sorry I asked," Laura began, not doubting for a moment that she would be, "but what would you do if you were in my place?"

Do I really want to know?

"Simple. I'd get on that modem and ask for a face-to-face meeting—preferably over dinner, or drinks at the very least, at some dark, cozy *très* intimate place," Zara replied with certainty.

"I was right," Laura said, rolling her eyes skyward. "I *am* sorry I asked!"

"How would you feel about dinner and a movie?"

Ben smiled to himself. How long now had he been thinking exactly the same thing? "You must be reading my mind. I was just about to order a pizza and pop a videocassette into the old VCR." *Just in case she wasn't making an entirely serious suggestion,* he decided.

"That's not exactly what I had in mind."

Good! "Oh?" he asked.

"No. I was thinking that perhaps you and I could do something."

You must have been reading my mind! "Together?" he wanted to know.

"Well, yes, that *was* the general idea."

Excellent idea. "Are you asking me out, Unhappily?"

"That's about the size of it."

This is a switch. "Very funny!"

"I thought so."

And a relief. "Are you serious?" he asked.

"I was when I asked. Now I'm not so sure."

Uh-oh. "Well, if the offer still stands, the answer is yes."

"Are you sure?"

Am I sure? Do fish swim? "Sure I'm sure. You took me by surprise, that's all. I've never had a woman ask me out before," he admitted.

"Never?"

I've never even had a woman make a pass at me. "Absolutely never. I told you, I married the girl next door, the only one I ever loved or even dated," he typed.

"I'm new at this, too, Misery. It would seem we're a couple of babes in the woods when it comes to dating," she told him.

It could be worse, but I don't know how. "Pitiful, aren't we?"

"To say the least."

Now for the next step. "When?"

"What?"

"When would you like to get together?" he asked.

"Soon."

Progress. This is good. "Sounds good to me."

"All right. You pick a date."

Me? Why me? "This Friday."

"That'll work."

Next step. "Any place special you'd like to go?"

"I'll have to think about that."

Great. How can I suggest anything if I don't know where she lives? "Okay, I'll narrow things down a bit. Any particular *city?*"

"How about Chicago?" she asked.

Chicago? Laura lives in Chicago. "Chicago? Why Chicago?"

"Well, there *is* a lot to do in Chicago. A lot of fine restaurants."

But I might bump into my ex-wife.

"Yeah, I guess you're right."

"You don't seem wildly enthusiastic."

Chicago's definitely not my kind of town. "It's not that."

"Let me guess. A country boy who has a major aversion to big cities."

That's a classic understatement. "Something like that, yeah."

"Would you prefer to meet somewhere in the suburbs? Closer to where you live, wherever that is?"

Anywhere else, actually. The moon would be nice. "No. Chicago's fine. Not that long a drive, actually."

"Are you sure?"

No. I'm not sure at all. But what can I say? "Yeah."

"I don't mind meeting someplace else."

Diplomacy, Westin. Diplomacy. "Chicago's fine."

"All right. Let me think about this and get back to you tomorrow with the names of some restaurants."

With my luck, they'll include Laura's favorites. "Sounds good to me." He thought about it, about her. Then after a momentary hesitation, he added: "(((O)))"

"What's that?"

"Let's just call it a cyberhug."

A cyberhug. I rather like that.

Laura was at once nervous and elated. She'd made the first move. She'd asked him out, and it had worked. He'd accepted. Though she wanted it to happen, she still felt ambivalent. She told herself it was normal under the circumstances, but . . .

We're finally going to meet.

But what if it turned out to be a disaster? What if they didn't like each other? What if he was disappointed? What if she was disappointed? What if he was as old as dirt and just as ugly? What if all of those shallow, superficial things meant more to her in the end than even she realized?

What if . . .

What if I'm worrying myself to death for nothing?

Even if he *was* old and ugly, so what? He obviously had a beautiful soul. A wonderful soul. A caring soul. Did it matter what the exterior looked like? What could she do about it if it did? *Should* it matter?

No.

It didn't matter. It didn't matter at all. She told herself she didn't care, but that wasn't entirely true. She wanted him to match her vision of him. She wanted it more than she was willing to admit.

What if he didn't?

I'll bet she's beautiful.

How could she be anything but?

Ben thought about it. He'd thought about it so many times since their first on-line encounter. He envisioned her as an incredibly beautiful, sexy, vital woman—not, surprisingly, unlike Laura. This came as a surprise to him because it seemed that the last thing he should want would be a woman who looked like Laura.

That would be incredibly stupid, actually.

I must be nuts.

That had to be the understatement of the year. He wondered if he should be wearing one of those Kick Me signs on his backside. After all the pain his marriage to Laura had brought him, why on earth would he fantasize about another woman just like her?

Because, like it or not, she still mattered to him.

Was that stupid, or what?

"We can't help who we fall in love with," his mother told him.

He frowned. "Can we help being stupid?" he asked sullenly.

He hoped not. He would like to think he couldn't help it.

"Not always, no."

"Both are genetic defects, is that it?" He poured himself a cup of coffee, then proceeded to ignore it.

I can hope, can't I?

"No, they're *human* defects," his mother responded patiently. "We all have them."

"Maybe eventually, someone will come up with a cure," Ben said with mock hopefulness.

"Losing Laura hurt because you loved her," Emily reminded him.

That made sense. "No kidding."

"Let me finish, Benjamin," she said firmly. "You've been hurting since the divorce, I know. I always thought—hoped—the two of you would get back together, but since that doesn't seem to be in the cards, I'm pleased that you've finally met someone." The look on her face, the optimism in her voice told him she really meant it—but then, knowing his mother, she wouldn't have said it if she didn't mean it.

How do I explain this one to her? "I haven't exactly met her, Mom," he admitted. "We've been writing or communicating or whatever you want to call it, by computer." He could only imagine how that must sound to his very traditional, old-fashioned mother.

"You obviously find her attractive." If she was concerned—or surprised—by his very admission, she didn't show it.

I don't know if she is or not, actually.

"What I know of her *is* attractive," he acknowledged. It was the truth. Her words, her statements, her attitudes *were* attractive. Very attractive.

"That's a start."

Not much of one, but yeah, it's a start.

"Yeah, I suppose so."

But would it be enough?

Here goes nothing, Laura thought anxiously. "Do you like Italian?"

"I love Italian."

She gave an inward sigh of relief. "Wonderful. I discovered this delightful little Italian restaurant a couple of months ago—Florentine, actually. It's cozy, great ambience."

"Sounds good."

He's game. That's good. "Better than good. You'll see."

"I can't wait."

He's being polite. "I'm glad to hear it."

"You've never been to Italy?"

I wish. "No, but I'd like to. Why do you ask?"

"You said the restaurant was Florentine. Not many people differentiate by region."

Observant. A good sign. "I do, just as I would a Chinese restaurant."

"My ex-wife did, too."

Not Ben. Never Ben. "My ex-husband didn't."

"See what I mean?"

Not really. "Vaguely."

"Would you like to take in a movie afterward?"

"Depends. What do you have in mind?"

"Well, I'm not familiar with the Chicago cinemas, but I'm sure we can find an acceptable compromise."

There's a word I haven't heard in a while. "Compromise?"

"I like action, you like romance. We could see a comedy."

"Now that's what I call a compromise."

"I thought so."

"I'm sure. How about Friday? Seven-thirty?"

It wasn't until after they had signed off that Laura realized she hadn't given him her name or even described herself to him.

I've made a date with the man and didn't even tell him my name, she thought. *I'm still holding back.*

But then, so is he.

Ben was getting cold feet. *That was putting it mildly.*

Here he was, about to go out on his first date at his age. His first date with someone other than Laura.

Was he ready for it?

He'd told himself over and over again that he was. He wanted to be ready. He *needed* to be ready, because anything was better than the misery of the past year, missing Laura and wanting her and hoping against hope that one day soon they'd get back together. Anything was better than the loneliness, the feeling of isolation.

Maybe, maybe not.

And knowing, deep down, that it wasn't going to happen.

He believed Unhappily Unwed—or whoever she really was—could be the woman to make him forget Laura.

So why was he suddenly having doubts now?

Am I just making excuses? he asked himself. *Am I so unwilling to let go of Laura that I can't bring myself to get on with my life?*

He wondered if anyone could be that stupid.

I could, he decided.

He apparently was.

The more he thought about it, the more certain he was that things were moving too fast, that he really wasn't ready for a new relationship.

This wasn't a new relationship. This was just dinner—and maybe a movie.

He was making too much of it.

Wasn't he?

But he still wasn't ready.

* * *

It was too soon, Laura decided.

Way too soon.

She'd given it a great deal of thought—in fact, she'd thought of little else since making the date.

We're moving too fast, she told herself. *I'm moving too fast.*

She'd been so enthusiastic at the time. She was curious. She was intrigued by him. She *wanted* to meet him, to learn more about him.

But was she ready for another relationship?

It wasn't really a relationship, she told herself. *Not yet, anyway.*

But it could be.

If she let it.

Would she?

She didn't know the answer to that. She wasn't sure how she felt, what she wanted.

That could change after they met.

But she wasn't sure it was a change she was ready for.

Should I cancel? she wondered.

8

"**I** can't make it."

That sounded so cold.

Ben hated himself for doing this, but it had to be done. He wasn't ready. Going through with this "date" now, feeling as he did, would be a disaster.

"I'm sorry to hear that," came Laura's surprisingly calm response.

"I've got relatives coming in from out of town." He hated lying to her like this. "They decided to come sooner than expected."

This is really lame. "Those things happen, Misery. It's all right. I was going to have to cancel myself anyway. I have to go on a business trip."

I'll bet you do. "Rain check, then?"

"Of course."

She was going to cancel. *She* didn't want to have dinner with *him* after extending the invitation. He thought about it after they'd signed off. She probably didn't have to go on a business trip at all.

She'd just changed her mind, that was all.

It was clear to Ben now that this wasn't going to work, would never have worked. It just wasn't in the cards. He should have known better. He should have known from the start.

I was a fool to think there was any hope for a relationship with a woman I met by computer, he told himself.

I should have known better, Laura reprimanded herself.

I shouldn't have listened to Zara.

She should have known that a relationship with a man she'd met via computer network didn't have a snowball's chance in hell of working. *There's still just one way to meet Mr. Right.*

The conventional way.

But then, *that* way hadn't worked for her, either.

She stared at the blank computer screen, wondering what *would* work for her. Not this, obviously.

Could Ben possibly have been right about her? *Was* she so wrapped up in her career that she no longer knew how to have an intimate relationship?

Was it *her* fault?

That's not exactly what he said, she recalled miserably. *He said I had no interest in an intimate relationship.*

That was the same as saying it was her fault.

Which wasn't true.

Was it?

Sometimes she had to wonder.

She'd met so many attractive men since the divorce, but she'd kept all of them at arm's length. She'd been asked out, but always politely declined. Misery Loves Company had been safe because he was just words on a computer screen—not flesh and blood, not even a name.

But if they had met, all of that would change.

Did she *want* that?

Ben knew she was beautiful, even though he couldn't see her face.

She's incredible, he thought as he watched her.

She was wearing a mask, an elaborate mask of sequins and feathers, turquoise and silver to match her dress. He couldn't see her face, but he could see her hair. It was long and lush, an all-too-familiar pale shade of ash blond.

Laura's hair.

She extended her arms to him. She wanted him to dance with her. He obliged without hesitation, taking her in his arms. As he glided across the floor, holding her close, he stroked her hair, finding its silkiness strangely comforting. Her perfume, too, was a scent he recognized.

Laura's perfume.

"I want to make love with you," he told her.

How much he wanted that!

She didn't speak, but nodded.

I want you so much, I can't stand it!

He reached for the mask, but she stopped him, shaking her head emphatically. "All right, we'll do it your way," he said. His arms around her again, he unzipped the back of her sequined dress and allowed it to slide off her shoulders and down the length of her body to the floor.

He caught his breath. *Beautiful.*

She wore nothing beneath the dress. He scooped her up and carried her to a blue velvet sofa, where she lay watching him in silence as he undressed.

Familiar. So familiar...

He knelt beside the sofa and kissed her deeply, hungrily. She returned the kiss eagerly. They touched each other, explored each other's bodies unhurriedly with lips and hands. They came together, joined physically, passionately, only when neither of them could wait any longer.

Incredible...

Only afterward would she allow him to remove the mask.

It was Laura...

Ben woke with a start.

Laura.

The dream had seemed so real. She was there, and they were making love as they had then, before everything started to go wrong between them. Making love the way they used to when things were so good between them, when they were so crazy in love.

When they were happy together.

Why couldn't he let it go?

Laura lay back in a tub full of warm water and fragrant bubbles, her eyes closed, the warmth and scent of jasmine and rose relaxing her. She closed her eyes, grateful for the escape, however brief, from an unbearably hectic day. Her mind began to drift, to daydream . . .

She didn't recognize the man, but he was handsome. He was tall and dark, with the bluest eyes she'd ever seen. His smile was warm but sexy. He wore faded jeans but no shirt. He was tanned, muscular, a man who obviously spent a great deal of time outdoors.

It's him. It has to be.

"Misery?" she asked.

"Not anymore."

He was all she'd imagined he would be. "Good."

"Unhappy?"

Not a chance. Not anymore. "I used to be." That was the truth.

He took her in his arms. "Sorry to hear it," he said. Then he kissed her deeply. "I hope you never will be again."

That makes two of us. "I won't be, as long as you're here." she told him. *Please don't leave. Not now, not ever.*

"Then you never will be again."

How much she wanted to believe that! "Don't make promises you can't—or won't—keep," she cautioned.

"Oh, I'll keep this one, all right," he assured her.

"That's what my ex-husband said, too," she remembered. And look how that turned out.

"I'm not your ex-husband."

But in some ways he seemed so much like Ben. "Maybe not, but you are human," she said. *At least I hope you are.*

"Are you sure about that?"

I wish I were. "We've never met before." She wasn't so sure about that....

"No— "Until now, all I've been to you has been a response on a computer screen," he pointed out.

She nodded, unable to argue with that. "No face, no name." *Just a fantasy,* she was thinking. Again she nodded.

"So how do you know I'm real?" he asked.

I don't.... She touched his arm. "Oh, you're real, all right," she said confidently. *Thank God!*

"I could be computer generated," he suggested.

No. That couldn't possibly be. "And you could be playing games with me," she observed.

"This is no game, I assure you." He kissed her again. "I just want you to be sure."

She was sure...so sure... "Of what?" she asked.

"Of me. Of us," he said.

If only he knew how sure she was. "I'm sure. I'm as sure as I'll ever be," she promised him.

"You don't really know me," he reminded her.

Yes, I do. I feel as if I've known you all my life. "I know all I need to know." That was the truth.

"Are you sure?"

"I'm sure." As sure as she'd ever be.

"In that case..." He slowly unbuttoned her silk shirt, his hands lingering on her breasts.

She was on fire....

"Let's make love," she whispered hoarsely.

Please, now... now...

"Patience," he said with a lazy smile. He unhooked her lacy white bra and pushed it back, exposing her. She could hear his breath catch in his throat. "You *are* beautiful, Laura," he gasped.

He made her beautiful with his love.

"I feel beautiful," she responded.

"You are. So, so beautiful..."

"You make me feel beautiful." *Love me. Just love me.*

"I love you."

"I love you, too."

They came together eagerly, and it was unlike anything she'd ever experienced before...

Laura's thoughts returned to the present abruptly. She could hear her heart thudding wildly within her chest, and she was trembling.

If only it could really be like that, she thought.

It was just a dream, Ben kept telling himself.

An incredible, wonderful dream.

It would never be like that again. Not for him and Laura.

Never again...

What about the other woman in his life? What about Unhappily Unwed?

Is she really a part of my life? he asked himself. *Or have I already shut her out?*

Had he made a mistake by canceling their date?

More important than that, was it one he could correct?

You're a fool, Westin.

She'd seemed so right for him—more so, actually, than Laura had ever been. He wanted to meet her, he really did, but the specter of Laura stood between them.

Laura. Always Laura.

Why? Why did he *let* her interfere with his life?

The truth was, she'd been standing between him and happiness with or without anyone else since the day she left Fowler Falls. But just being aware of that fact wasn't enough.

Unfortunately.

I had doubts. Why am I angry at him because he has doubts?

It was stupid. Very stupid. She'd had to admit it. She was angry at him for having doubts when she'd had them herself.

Dumb, dumb dumb!

Why couldn't he have at least been honest with her?

Was that too much to ask?

But then, *I wasn't honest with him, was I? I made excuses, too, didn't I?*

She certainly had. She was scared, too.

Insecure was more like it.

So why had she been so hard on him? Why had she been so defensive when he canceled their date?

Because I'm an idiot, that's why.

Could it have been the sting of rejection that made her defensive?

Very possibly, she thought. *Very possibly.*

She suddenly felt like a fool.

"I hope you're not too ticked at me," Ben typed. *You have every right to be.*

"Ticked?" she asked.

"Yeah. You know—angry." *I would be if I were you.*

"No, of course not. Why would I be?" she wanted to know.

Why wouldn't you be? "Well, you know. For canceling." *For being a world-class jerk.*

"You did have a good reason for doing so," she said.

Wanna bet? "I know. But I feel bad about it just the same." *To put it mildly.*

"Thank you for that."

"Huh?" Now he really felt like a jerk.

"It's nice to know you do feel badly about not being able to keep our date," she told him.

You have no idea. "You thought I wouldn't?" he asked.

"I wasn't sure," she admitted.

"Well, I did." *An understatement.*

"I appreciate your honesty," she said.

That stung. Probably because he hadn't been completely honest with her.

"Are you still there, Misery?"

I'm looking for a razor blade. "Yeah, I'm here. I was just thinking, that's all." *Hold on while I go slit my wrists.*

"A penny for your thoughts, at the risk of sounding cliché," she told him.

"You'd be throwing your money away."

"I'll bet."

"It's true."

"You just don't want to tell me what you were thinking."

You got that right. "That's not true."

"All right, then—'fess up, Misery."

"Okay. I was thinking about how important honesty is in a relationship." *I was thinking about what a heel I am.*

"Unfortunately, too many of us don't realize that until it's too late."

Us? "Us—as in yourself included?"

"As much as I hate to admit it. Yes."

What is this, anyway—True Confessions? "I guess we're in the same boat, then."

"You, too?"

Definitely. "The road to divorce court is paved with little white lies."

"I don't doubt that."

We're living proof of that, aren't we? "I have to be straight with you, Unhappily."

"I should hope so."

"I didn't have anybody coming in from out of town." *She's going to be furious, and I don't blame her.*

"Oh?"

At least she can't find me to kill me. "No. I lied." *Or can she?*

"So did I," she responded.

"What?"

"I didn't have to go out of town on business," she confessed.

What? "No?" he asked. *She lied, too?*

"No."

Now I don't feel so guilty. "Why'd you say you did?" he wanted to know.

"Why did you say you had relatives coming to visit?"

Hey! "I didn't want to admit I'd had cold feet," he said.

"Neither did I."

Ben laughed with relief and wondered how to express laughter on the computer screen. "Ha Ha."

"Are you laughing at me, Misery?" she asked.

"No, I'm laughing at *us.*" It was the truth.

"We *are* pretty ridiculous."

That was for sure. "That we are," he agreed.

"So we both suffered from last-minute stage fright."

"So it would seem."

"Apparently."

This was going nowhere fast. "I hope it's not going to prevent us from pursuing our relationship further," he said, concerned.

If we survive this, we can deal with anything. "I hope not."

"Shall we make another date, then?" Would she ever want to meet him after this?

"Maybe we should slow down, give it a little time. I think we'll both know when the time is right to meet."

Ben smiled to himself. She'd taken the bytes right out of his mouth. Then, impulsively, he typed one more thing.

"((((0))))"

Another hug.

9

They were both being cautious. That was understandable.

Laura thought about it as she sat alone in a large conference room high above the city of Chicago, waiting for her colleagues to assemble for an important meeting. They'd both been burned—badly. Being cautious in a new relationship wasn't such a bad idea. In fact, it was a good idea. She didn't think she could endure another failed relationship. She couldn't go through what she'd gone through with Ben—not again.

She just couldn't take it.

A new relationship, she thought. He'd called it a relationship. When she stopped to think about it, what else could it be called, whether traditional or via computer? It might be a bit unorthodox, but it was nonetheless a relationship.

It is still a relationship, she told herself, *such as it is.*

Even if they'd never met, even if they didn't know each other's names. No matter how crazy it might have seemed in the beginning, it was a growing, even promising, relationship.

"What planet are you on today?"

Laura looked up. Zara was arranging bound documents and pens at each seat at the long table. "Planet?" Laura asked.

Zara nodded, grinning. "I was just wondering which one you were on. It certainly wasn't Earth."

If she only knew.

Laura shook her head. "I was just thinking about this meeting," she lied. She really didn't want to get into this, not right now and not with Zara. Definitely not with Zara.

She'd never let her off the hook.

"I didn't think this one was going to be anything major," Zara said, mildly puzzled. She didn't look as if she believed a word of it.

She probably doesn't.

"It isn't really," Laura told her, "but it is *my* presentation."

That much, at least, was true.

"True."

At least we agree on something.

Laura glanced at the documents now lining the table. "You *did* go over them—" she asked, suddenly concerned.

As if she had to ask.

"Word by word," Zara assured her. "They're flawless, like everything else I do." There was no false modesty there. Zara was good. Zara was the best, in fact—and she knew it.

Unfortunately, that estimation also extended to her perceptive skills.

Laura made a face. "You're so modest," she teased.

"I'm not bragging, just stating fact," Zara said with a shrug. Then she pulled up a chair, sat backward on it and leaned against the back. "The masses won't start filing in for a while yet. How're things going with your mystery man?"

Laura's luck had just run out.

"Mystery man?"

Play dumb.

"Yeah, you know—Cyberhunk," Zara prompted to refresh Laura's memory.

Cyberhunk?

Laura laughed. "Zara, for all I know, he could be four-foot-two, six hundred pounds and wearing thick glasses," she pointed out. *Or worse,* she told herself.

Zara howled with laughter. "What an image!" she hooted.

"It's possible."

Unfortunately.

"Not humanly," Zara assured her.

But Laura knew, at this point, that just about anything was possible.

"Where's your head today, big brother?" Ray wanted to know.

If he only knew, Ben thought.

"Huh?" He decided to play dumb.

"Wherever it is, it's not on work," Ray observed, nodding toward the detailing Ben had been working on. Not only was it not the right color, the same as the other side, it was also uneven.

Fortunately, he doesn't know.

Only now did Ben realize with horror that he'd used the wrong color paint. Releasing a very loud expletive, he scrambled to his feet and banged a fist against the vehicle's hood. How could he have done anything so stupid?

That was easy. His mind wasn't on his work.

"You must have been daydreaming," Ray offered, as if reading his mind.

Something like that.

"Obviously."

"X-rated or R."

R, he was thinking.

"G," Ben told him.

"You used the wrong paint because of a dull daydream?"

Ben grinned. "Sorry to disappoint you, little brother."

If he only knew.

He wasn't about to tell Ray—or Sam either, for that matter—what he'd been thinking. That was just what he *didn't* need—his brothers grilling him further about the new woman in his life.

The new woman in his life?

The new woman in my life, he thought. *I do like the sound of that. It's been a long time since I had a woman in my life.*

If only he could get Laura out of his system, once and for all.

If only he could shake his own ambivalence about this new woman, this new relationship.

Relationship.

If only he could be sure.

I was sure of Laura.

If only... But you could never really be sure about anyone or anything in life. He'd been sure about Laura, and look where that had gotten him. A one-way ticket to Heartbreak Hotel.

To put it mildly.

He wished he could forget, but he couldn't.

"We really do have a lot in common, Misery," Laura started off. *We're both chicken,* she was thinking.

"I thought we'd already established that."

"I'm talking about cowardice." *How will he take that?*

"Cowardice?"

"Yes. It would seem that we both tend to lean toward the color yellow." *Don't approach this too seriously. Treat it like a joke.*

"How do you figure?"

"Easy. We had plans, remember? We were finally going to meet." *Remember that?*

"Yeah ... go on."

"We both got cold feet," she pointed out.

"Acknowledged. So?" he asked.

"If that's not chicken, Misery, I don't know what is." *If we had feathers, we could pluck 'em.*

"You're doing wonders for my ego here, sweetheart," he confessed.

"Sweetheart?" *Sweetheart? Is that a typo, or what?*

There was a moment's hesitation before his answer came.

"Yeah," he typed.

"I'm touched."

"Good. I'd hoped you would be."

"Here I am, trying to be glib, and you throw me a curve like that."

"Is that how you see it? A curve?" he asked.

"In a way," she admitted. *In a big way, actually.*

"Why?"

"It took me by surprise." *For lack of a better way to put it.*

"Really?"

"Yes. You've never done it before." *Never.*

"There's a first time for everything, after all."

"True, very true," she agreed. *For both good things and bad.*

"And I just felt like it," he confessed.

"It would suggest affection." *Or something more.*

"It surprises you that I could feel affection for you?" he asked.

"Not that you *could*, that you *do*."

"Well, I do—more than you know."

And the feeling's mutual, she thought as she contemplated her response. *More than you know.*

Why had he done that? Why had he called her sweetheart?

Ben was just as surprised as she had been. It certainly wasn't premeditated. He hadn't planned it, hadn't even thought about it until he heard the word coming out of his mouth—or rather, saw the word being typed on his screen.

Sweetheart. He'd called her "sweetheart." Until that moment, he'd never called anyone but Laura that.

Laura's the past, he reprimanded himself. *I have to get her out of my system. I have to forget her.*

He was beginning to think he should have gone through with it, kept that first date they'd made. That was the key, the first step to getting on with his life—seeing other women.

Getting involved with other women.

Forgetting Laura, if he could.

Maybe even falling in love again.

And he *did* have feelings for this new woman in his life. Even though they'd never met, even though he didn't know her name or what she looked like, he had strong feelings for her.

Could that possibly grow into love?

He felt as though he *did* know her in all the ways that counted.

Sweetheart.

He'd called her "sweetheart."

Did he mean anything by it?

Laura told herself not to make too much of it. Lots of people called everybody "honey" and "sweetheart" more out of habit than endearment.

Men, especially.

But he wasn't lots of people.

Who is he?

And she was sure he wasn't the type to use such terms of endearment loosely.

She didn't know *how* she was sure, but she was.

Not him, she thought with certainty.

She wasn't sure exactly why she was so certain of that, but she was.

I'm not even making sense to me!

Ben was like that, she remembered now. He'd never been the type to call a stranger—or even a family friend—"honey" or "sweetie."

Except her.

He'd always called her "darling" and "honey" and "sweetheart." Was that why this was so significant to her now? Or was it just wishful thinking on her part?

Was she hearing what she wanted to hear?

Am I making too much of it? she asked herself now

* * *

"Shall we take another shot at it?" Ben held his breath and waited for her reply.

"At what?"

"Dinner, of course." *For starters.*

"You really want to?" she asked.

"I wouldn't ask if I didn't." *I almost didn't ask even though I do.*

"I don't know about that."

"Yeah, well, I wouldn't—*especially* after last time," he assured her.

"Neither would I, now that you mention it," she replied.

"Where would you like to go?" *Let her choose.*

"How about the same restaurant I suggested last time?" she asked.

"Perfect. We can have a late dinner after the concert." He checked to make sure he still had the address. *See how she feels about it.*

"Concert?"

"Yeah. Dakota Law and Chelsea Stone are going to be in town, and yours truly has tickets. Two of the best seats in the house." *Something for both of us.*

"Sounds wonderful—but could we make it dinner first, then the concert?" she asked.

"Your wish is my command." *Literally.*

"Right."

"What time?" he asked.

"Sixish?"

"No problem. Want to meet at the restaurant?"
Probably the safest route to take.

"That would probably be best."

"See you then...."

"Ben's got a date," Sam guessed.

Great, Ben thought. *It's starting already.* He wished they would leave him alone and let him work.

"How do you figure?" Ray wanted to know.

"He was late coming in this morning."

Don't make mountains out of molehills, you two.

"So?"

"He went to the cleaners."

"I repeat, so?"

You took the words right out of my mouth, little brother.

"He took his suit to be cleaned."

"Which one?"

"He's only got one, stupid."

That's right—rub it in.

"Oh, that's right."

"Who do you think he could be seeing?"

None of your business.

"Probably the computer lady."

"Computer lady?"

"Yeah, you know—the one he's been talking to on that computer of his."

Ignore them and they'll go away.

"Think it's serious?"

"Could be, I guess."

If you only knew—but I'm glad you don't!

"Wonder what she looks like."

"I shudder to think."

They leaned against a wall in the garage, watching Ben as he worked. Up to that point, he'd ignored them, ignored their good-natured ribbing. Now he stopped what he was doing and looked up at them, mildly annoyed. "Would you two please knock it off?" he asked, sucking in a deep breath. "I'm sure you both have work to do."

They were probably both behind.

"Well, yeah," Ray admitted.

"Then don't you think you should get to it?" Ben asked.

"I guess," Sam grumbled.

"Then get to it."

As the two retreated, Ben shook his head and chuckled to himself. They couldn't resist it. Those two would never be able to resist giving him a bad time. This had been going on since they were kids. He suspected it would probably continue well into old age.

He was as curious as they were about the lady, though he'd never tell Sam and Ray that. *No point in giving them ammunition,* he decided. They had plenty of their own.

It promised to be an interesting evening, at the very least.

* * *

"Way to go!" Zara cheered.

Zara's response was predictable. Laura only smiled. "I'm glad you approve."

"Approve?" Zara hooted. "I say it's about time!"

Laura saw no reason to tell her that she felt exactly the same way. It was overtime. In fact, it was overdue.

"When's the big event?" Zara wanted to know.

The big event? "What?" Laura asked.

"When are you seeing him?"

"Friday."

"Where?"

"Oh, no, you don't," Laura said with an emphatic wave of her hand. "I'm not looking for an audience, Zara."

She could imagine a cozy, romantic dinner by candlelight—and Zara and a dozen of her closest male admirers, with their faces pressed to the window, watching.

"Audience?" Zara wrinkled her nose disdainfully. "What audience? I'm only trying to help you."

"Help me what?" Laura gave her a skeptical look.

"Plan your evening, of course. Now, where are you going?"

"Dinner and a concert."

Keep it vague, Laura.

"Nice restaurant?"

"Cozy."

"Good, good. And the concert?"

"Country."

Zara looked genuinely surprised. "You like country?"

"It's a compromise," Laura admitted.

Another unfamiliar word.

"Yeah, okay," Zara said with a nod. "The important thing, now, is to get to the restaurant early so you can get a look at him before you commit yourself."

"Zara!" Laura tried to conceal her amusement.

"What's his name, anyway?"

Laura frowned. "I have no idea."

10

This was it, Ben told himself. This was the big day.

They were finally going to meet. For better or worse.

He was definitely looking forward to his first face-to-face meeting with Unhappily Unwed, but that certainly didn't stop him from being nervous.

Extremely nervous.

He thought about it now as he shaved. Standing naked, except for his briefs, in front of the bathroom mirror, the face that started back at him was decidedly vulnerable. It was then that he realized that he had never been out on a date with anyone but Laura—and even then, there had been no surprises because they'd known each other forever.

Or so he'd thought at the time.

It was like going out for the evening with an old friend, he recalled, _because that's exactly what Laura was. An old friend._

She used to be, anyway.

Back then, he'd believed there was nothing he didn't know about Laura, that there was nothing new left for him to discover.

At least there was nothing he'd wanted to discover.

Boy, was I ever wrong! he told himself now.

This time, it would be different.

Tonight, he decided, would be full of surprises. He was having dinner with a woman he'd never met before, at least not in the physical sense. He didn't know what she looked like. He didn't even know her name.

Does it matter?

He'd asked for her name, but she'd declined. He wondered if this was her way of playing it safe. Did she plan to get to the restaurant early so she could get a look at him before she decided whether or not to stick around?

Most likely she would.

Ben smiled to himself. *If so, we're on the same wavelength.*

He was planning to do exactly the same thing.

Sneaky, but human.

Not that physical appearance was all that important to him—she'd have to be an old hag to put enough of a damper on his curiosity to drive him away now.

An old hag—literally.

Even then it might not matter.

Sam and Ray were absolutely right—for once. He needed to put Laura and their failed marriage behind him and get on with his life. He needed to find someone else.

Easier said than done, he admitted, but only to himself.

But tonight would definitely be a step in the right direction.

I can't believe I'm doing this.

Was she desperate, or what?

Laura had never been on a blind date before—actually, she'd never been on any kind of a date with anyone other than Ben. *Maybe that was the problem,* she told herself now. *Maybe we should have both gone out with others before we got married.*

Maybe they needed a basis for comparison.

At the time, though, there hadn't seemed to be a need for that—on her part or his. *We loved each other,* Laura remembered. *We needed no basis for comparison.*

But times changed. People changed. She'd finally managed to put the past behind her. Tonight was going to be the first step toward her future without Ben. She was finally going to put Ben and all that had gone wrong between them behind her.

She was going to try, anyway.

With a little help from my friend, she thought.

And Misery Loves Company *was* a friend, even if she hadn't yet met him face-to-face. He understood her as no other man, not even Ben—especially not Ben—ever had. He had made her see that there were men out there who were caring and considerate, men who weren't threatened by a woman's ambitions or successes.

Renaissance men.

Men she could have a satisfying relationship with.

Men who would respect her drive and ambition.

She muttered an expletive under her breath as she spotted a run in her new stocking. This was definitely not a good omen, she decided as she went to her bureau for another pair. While putting them on, she discovered a large chip in her nail polish.

What next?

Disaster comes in threes, she recalled as she attempted to repair the chip. *What's next?*

What else could—would—go wrong?

She wasn't sure she wanted to know.

She didn't even want to think about it.

She didn't want anything to go wrong tonight. Tonight was the start of a whole new life for her. Whatever happened—or didn't happen—tonight with Misery Loves Company, it was a start.

A good start.

It was the first step in putting the pain of the past behind her, once and for all.

An important step.

It was difficult to admit, even to herself, but Laura had high hopes for tonight. She hoped he lived up to her mental image of him. She wanted him to be her Mr. Right. It wasn't that she was desperate to have a man in her life—if that were the case, she would have taken at least one of the opportunities for romantic involvement that had been presented to her since the divorce. She just wanted to prove to herself that she could have a successful relationship, that she could have a relationship with someone other than Ben.

A meaningful relationship.

And Misery seemed so right for her.

But then, so had Ben.

As she left her apartment and heard the lock click, she realized she could stop worrying about that third disaster.

Her keys were still inside.

Is she here yet? Ben wondered.

Was she watching him at that very moment?

He scanned the restaurant, wondering if any of the women already present might be Unhappily Unwed. He smiled to himself at the mental image that thought evoked.

Unhappily Unwed.

Probably at least half of them, he decided.

"May I help you, sir?"

He definitely needed help.

"Sir?"

The hostess took him by surprise. "Huh?"

"May I help you?" she repeated the question.

"I'm not sure," he began slowly. "I'm supposed to meet someone here. A woman."

She'd probably already guessed as much.

The hostess nodded, turning to her reservation book. "Her name?"

Trick question. "Uh—I don't really know," Ben confessed. *I must sound like a real moron.*

She gave him a puzzled look. "I see," she said. But it was clear that she really didn't.

A world-class moron.

Ben craned his neck, continuing to look around.

Was she here?

"If you'll tell me what she looks like, then—"

"I don't know that, either." *I feel so stupid.*

Now the hostess was really confused.

That made two of them.

Ben smiled. "We've never really met," he explained. "We've been communicating through one of those computer networks—you know, using handles instead of names—"

"Oh!" The hostess brightened. "Just a moment, please."

She is here!

Referring again, this time briefly, to her reservation book, she gestured to him to follow her.

She must be here. But . . .

Now it was Ben's turn to be confused. "She told you—"

"She told me you're Misery Loves Company," the hostess said, amused.

His face flushed.

"Swell."

She smiled.

"I think it's incredibly romantic," she told him.

Where is she?

He nodded. "Is she already here?"

She must be, surely.

"Yes—she arrived just a few moments before you did," the hostess explained.

He was right.

So much for getting a peek at her before she knows I'm here, Ben thought, no longer concerned. *I've waited a long time—or it's seemed like a long time, anyway—for this. I'm not going to back out now.*

For better or worse.

"Here he is," the hostess announced.

Hopefully not worse.

As she stepped aside to allow him to seat himself, Ben stopped in his tracks.

He couldn't believe his eyes.

"Is this some kind of bad joke?" he demanded angrily.

Laura!

"What are you doing here?" Laura wanted to know, standing up abruptly.

What am I doing here? "I was just about to ask you the same question," he said tightly.

"I'm meeting someone," she informed him.

So she was dating again. *Why do I care?*

"So am I!"

"Why here?" Laura demanded hotly.

"My date suggested it!"

"Does the poor woman know what she's getting herself into?"

He felt like a jealous husband.

"I could ask your date the same question—if he hasn't already bailed out!" Ben shot back at her.

That was low.

Now the hostess was really confused. "Excuse me—" she began, attempting to intervene.

This is a mistake.

"Please take me to my own table," Ben said then.

It has to be a mistake.

"This *is* your table," the hostess said in a feeble voice.

No mistake.

Laura shook her head. "There must be some mistake," she insisted.

"I'm afraid not," the hostess said regretfully.

How could this be happening?

They responded simultaneously. *"What?"*

Denial. That's what this is.

The hostess looked at Laura almost apologetically. "You told me you were expecting a man you'd never met, a man you knew only as Misery Loves Company."

Ben watched, waiting for her response.

Laura nodded.

Tame enough.

The woman turned to Ben. "And you said the lady you came to meet was someone you only knew via a computer network."

Right. This doesn't look too good. Ben nodded. Couldn't deny it any longer.

"Are you Misery Loves Company?"

Bingo. He nodded again.

"I don't believe it!" Laura gasped.

You don't believe it? "That makes two of us!" Ben hissed.

And they both stormed out of the restaurant.

It was like a bad dream.

Ben was Misery Loves Company? No—that simply was not possible.

A nightmare.

Was it?

It had to be.

No, she couldn't believe it, *wouldn't* believe it. Misery was a warm, sensitive, caring man.

He couldn't be Ben.

The kind of man she used to think her ex-husband was.

Ben was selfish and narrow-minded.

Misery respected her ambitions. Misery admired her independence.

The way she'd once believed Ben would.

Misery *cared.* He cared about her feelings, her needs.

The way Ben should have. The way Ben used to.

Misery was different. Misery was everything she used to think her ex-husband was.

Everything she'd hoped he would be. Everything he turned out not to be.

It couldn't be.

Was it possible? she asked herself as she drove home.

No!

She couldn't believe it.

Ben couldn't comprehend the situation.

Laura?

Laura was Unhappily Unwed? *Unhappy While Wed would be more like it,* he thought bitterly.

She'd never really been happy with him.

How could he have been taken in by her? How could he have been so easily fooled? How could he not have known this was his ex-wife?

How could he have not seen through her?

That's easy, he told himself. *I didn't see it because I didn't want to see it.*

Because I was a fool.

And because Laura didn't want me to see it.

No wonder she didn't want to tell me her name before we met.

Now it all made sense.

Did she know it was me she was communicating with? he wondered.

Could this have been deliberate on her part?

No... no, that's not possible. She couldn't have known.

Could she?

* * *

Never again, Laura promised herself.

This had been a big mistake.

She should have known better.

Hadn't she told Zara as much? Hadn't she, when her assistant urged her to "give it a try," told Zara that it wasn't for her, that it wasn't her style?

She shouldn't have listened to Zara.

Why hadn't she stuck to her guns on that one?

But then, this wasn't really Zara's fault.

Why did she let her curiosity get the better of her?

It was her own fault. And Ben's.

That old cliché is true, she thought now. *Curiosity really does kill the cat.*

It doesn't do a hell of a lot for humans, either.

Ben.

He'd really put one over on her. He was probably having a good laugh about that now, she decided. She would bet he was enjoying every minute of stringing her along, making her believe she'd finally met someone she could care about, someone who might really care about her—someone who actually understood her and accepted her as she was.

She couldn't have been further from the truth.

Ben should have known better.

He did know better.

He'd never been into computers. He'd never even wanted to own one—when Laura had urged him to buy one, while they were still married, he had resisted. He wasn't technologically inclined, he'd told her then.

No computer was user-friendly to me, he recalled now.

It had taken him a while—a long while—to face the reality that a computer really could make life at the shop a lot easier. It had taken even longer for him to realize that it could make his private life a living hell.

How could he have been so stupid? he raged at himself. She was probably having a good laugh about this now.

For Laura, it proved to be a long and sleepless night.

She couldn't stop thinking about her encounter with Ben. Couldn't stop wondering how long he'd known *she* was Unhappily Unwed, how long he'd been playing his cruel little games with her.

How had he figured it out? she wondered. She'd been so careful—what had she done to give herself away? What had she told him that made him realize it was her?

Under normal circumstances, she would have concluded that he knew her so well, he'd recognize her no matter what.

But she'd realized a long time ago that Ben didn't know her at all.

Ben couldn't sleep, either.

It was the longest, most miserable night he'd had to

endure in a very long time. He couldn't stop thinking about that face-off with Laura. Couldn't stop wondering how long she'd known *he* was Misery Loves Company, how long she'd been playing this sick little game of hers.

How long had she known? he wondered. He'd been cautious, tried not to reveal anything identifying about himself until he knew more about her. What had he told her that tipped her off?

There was a time he wouldn't have had to wonder. He would have figured that she'd know him, no matter what.

But he'd known for a long time now that Laura didn't really know him at all.

11

"I should have known better." He spoke aloud, but to himself.

Sam gave Ben a suspicious look, wondering what was coming next. "About what?"

Startled, Ben jerked around, realizing for the first time that he wasn't alone in the garage. He reached for a rag, only to discover it was as grimy as his hands. "What? Oh, uh—I was just talking to myself. It's nothing."

He didn't want to talk about it.

"Didn't sound like nothing to me."

Especially not to either of his brothers.

"Well, it was."

"It's got something to do with your date last night, doesn't it?" Sam asked, unwilling to give up. His brothers enjoyed nothing more than prying into and speculating about his love life—or lack thereof.

They were downright nosy.

"There was no date."

That was the truth.

"Sure there was. You drove all the way to Chicago to meet that woman you've been talking to over the computer," Sam recalled. He didn't have to tell Ben that he and Ray had been more than a little curious.

Much more than a little.

"It never happened," Ben said tightly.

"She didn't show?"

Sam looked skeptical.

"She was there, all right—but there was no date." There was an iciness in his tone that matched the sudden temperature drop in his eyes.

Sam didn't take the hint.

"That bad?"

That bad! Ben almost laughed aloud.

"Worse."

"So you got there, saw she wasn't your type and split," Sam concluded.

"That pretty much covers it, yeah." *At least all I'm going to tell you.*

"Than why do I get the feeling there's more to it than that?"

Because there is.

"All right, you win. It was my ex." Laura's confession was reluctant to say the least.

"Your—*what?*" Zara's eyes bugged out.

"My ex-husband. Ben Westin." Why did she tell her?

Zara stared at Laura in disbelief. It was obvious that even though she'd pressed Laura to tell her all about the date that wasn't, what Laura had just revealed was probably the last thing Zara expected to hear. Zara, to whom almost nothing came as a surprise, was flabbergasted.

"You're kidding!" she gasped.

I wish I were. "Believe me, I never make jokes where my ex-husband is concerned," Laura assured her. She didn't really want to talk about it, but it was too late. The door had been opened—and she was the one who opened it. Unfortunately.

"So, what happened?"

A lot happened. And nothing happened. "Nothing happened." *Better to leave it at that.*

"Huh?"

Zara wasn't fooled.

"As soon as I realized Ben was the man I was supposed to meet, I got out of there as fast as I could," Laura explained, amazed that any explanation was necessary. She wondered if Zara would have stayed, had she suddenly found herself face-to-face with an ex-husband who'd hurt her that deeply.

Probably. Zara didn't scare easily.

But then, Zara probably would never allow herself to be placed at such a disadvantage.

Never in a million years.

"What did he do?"

He ruined my evening. He ruined my life. "I don't know. And I don't care." *Not entirely true.*

Zara didn't look convinced.

"I don't!" *Not true.*

"There's one thing I don't understand."

There's a great deal I don't understand. Laura gave her an annoyed look, but didn't respond. She had the feeling she already knew what was coming next.

Unfortunately.

"How did this happen anyway?"

"Beats the hell out of me."

Sam wasn't convinced.

"You wrote—or communicated or whatever they call it when computers are involved—to her for what—weeks, months?" Sam wanted to know. He looked as if he didn't believe a word of Ben's horror story.

"Something like that, yeah."

"And you had no idea this woman was Laura?"

"None whatsoever."

"How can that be?"

"Excuse me?"

"You and Laura grew up together. You were *married!*"

"Don't remind me." *As if I need to be reminded.*

"You two have to know each other better than most couples."

"Sometimes I wonder," Ben said sullenly. Most of the time he wondered.

"I'm serious, Benj."

Dead serious, Ben thought. *And unrelenting.* "So am I."

"How could you *not* know it was her?" Sam wanted to know.

Good question.

"That should be obvious," Ben said tightly. "Laura is and always has been an extremely clever woman. It probably wasn't hard at all for her to convince me she was someone else." It would have been much harder for him to believe—or admit—that he could have been so gullible.

So stupid.

"You never even suspected it was her?"

"I never had a clue."

Laura realized how absurd that must sound.

"Seriously?"

"If I had," Laura began tightly, "do you think I would have stayed in touch with him?"

"I don't know. Would you?"

I wish I knew. "Zara—"

"Come clean, Laura," Zara urged.

"About what?"

"Come *on* now," she pressured Laura. "Admit it!"

Laura's eyes narrowed suspiciously. "Admit *what?*" she wanted to know. She didn't like the sound of this.

"I've always suspected you still had the hots for your ex-husband."

"Oh, please!" *Let it go, Zara.*

"Are you denying it?"

Please let it go. "Yes, I'm denying it!"

"What if I said I don't believe you?"

"I'd tell you I don't care if you believe me or not." That was pretty much true.

"A little sensitive, aren't you?" Zara observed.

More than a little.

"Annoyed is more like it," Laura insisted. "Ben and I are divorced. The marriage didn't work. Whatever we did have together was over a long time ago."

Or it should have been, anyway.

Zara gave her a sly smile. "You sure about that?"

"Not for a moment," Ben insisted. He hadn't a clue, and that was the truth.

"That's weird." *To say the least.*

"Not really. Laura was careful. She never told me anything about herself that might have tipped me off." *She was smart. Too smart.*

"But you're sure she knew it was you on the other end of the line?"

Nobody was ever going to believe this.

"Well, yeah." He was sure.

"Why?"

"What?"

"Why are you so sure?"

"She *had* to know it was me!" That was the only possible explanation.

"Why?" Sam repeated.

Why, indeed. "Because, as you yourself have already said, we were married. We grew up together," Ben pointed out.

So why hadn't *he* known?

"You conveniently forgot that a minute ago," Sam pointed out.

So I did. "Yeah, well never mind that," Ben said with a dismissive wave of his hand. "*I* know that *she* knew it was me." He knew what was coming next.

"Didn't you do anything to conceal your identity?"

"Everything I could," Laura insisted.

She'd been careful, so careful.

"So he couldn't possibly have known, then," Zara concluded.

He shouldn't have, but he did. "That's what I thought—but apparently I was wrong," Laura said sullenly.

"If you didn't give him your name or tell him where you're from or where you're living now, how do you figure he knew it was you?"

"I don't know, but he knew." She was still sure of that.

"Did you ever tell him anything specific about your family?"

Never. "No."

"Your profession?"

Not a word. Laura shook her head.

"Then what makes you so sure he knew?" Zara asked.

He had to know. "I don't know. Maybe he guessed from my attitudes or whatever—but I'm sure he knew," Laura said with certainty. *Absolutely sure.*

"I think you're sure because at the moment you're angry and you *want* to be sure."

"That's not true!"

This was ridiculous.

"You sure about that?" Sam asked, unconvinced.

"Oh, come *on,* little brother," Ben snorted. "You think I would have divorced her if I still felt that way?" *If I were a fool I would—did.*

"Yeah."

"Then you must think I'm the high priest of morons." *Which I am.*

"No," Sam said, shaking his head, "but you *do* have too much pride for your own good."

"Meaning exactly what?" Ben asked carefully.

"Meaning you would have let Laura go before you'd admit to how much you were hurting."

True. And I couldn't. "Right," he said aloud.

"You can deny it till you're blue in the face, Benj, but *I* know *you,*" Sam reminded him. "It bruised your ego to have to share Laura with her career."

True. "I must be a real jerk," Ben grumbled.

"Sometimes you are, yeah."

"Do you really think I'm that narrow-minded?"

"When it comes to Laura you are."

Yes, I am. "I guess I shouldn't be so surprised that she found me so hard to live with, then."

"Not really."

Ben eyed him suspiciously.

"Why are you telling me all of this now?"

"Because I think you're still in love with him," Zara said firmly.

Laura laughed aloud at the thought. "Oh, please!"

"Do you deny it?"

"Yes, I deny it!" *But I've been denying it since the divorce.*

"Well, Laura Westin, you're *not* a very good liar," Zara informed her.

Yes. I am. "I beg your pardon?"

"Don't get yourself in an uproar—I haven't forgotten who signs my payroll," Zara assured her. "But I've gotten to know you, Laura. I'd like to think you're my friend as well as my boss—which means I can be honest with you."

As if she'd ever been anything but. "You have been so far. Brutally honest," Laura observed.

"I try to be."

"You'll be happy to know you're succeeding," Laura said sullenly. "What point, exactly, are you trying to make?" As if she didn't already know.

"I thought that was obvious."

Too obvious. "Enlighten me anyway."

"You still love the guy."

As much as she hated to admit it, she did. "Bull!"

"You *do*. That's why he gets to you."

"He gets to me because he's a royal pain in the—"

Zara shook her head, clucking disapprovingly. "He wouldn't get to you, no matter how much of a pain he might be, if you didn't *care* about him," she reasoned.

I guess I always have loved him. "Thank *you*, Dr. Freud." *And I always will.*

"Be serious, Laura."

"I *am* being serious," Laura maintained. "I lose my sense of humor when it comes to Benjamin Westin."

* * *

Ben was tempted to put his foot through the damn thing.

It had been nothing but trouble, anyway.

Ben glared contemptuously at the computer, as though it were a living, breathing being that could feel and understand his wrath. All of his anger and frustration and pain were focused on it; all of his rage at Laura was transferred to the machine. He wanted to smash it into a million pieces.

He wanted to destroy it.

Did he want to hit Laura? No... no matter how angry he was at her, he could never do *that*. But the thought of beating the bytes out of that infernal machine that had enabled her to so thoroughly humiliate him sure was tempting. In fact, it might give him some small degree of satisfaction to do just that. There was a symbolism there that was intensely appealing.

And necessary.

Almost too tempting, he thought.

As tempting, he decided, as the thought of punching his brother's lights out. Sam hadn't realized how close he came to that late today. Normally, his brothers' attempts to pry into his private affairs were annoying at most—but today Sam had crossed the line. His prying had become intolerable.

He'd gone too far.

Where did he get off telling him he was being bull-headed about admitting he was still in love with Laura? he thought angrily. Then he frowned to himself.

I am still in love with her.

The truth hurt.

Boy, did it hurt! he admitted, but only to himself.

It hurt because he did still love Laura. Loved her more than he could admit.

It hurt because she'd left him.

It hurt because he knew she had stopped loving him. She'd made a new life for herself, had probably never given him a thought.

It hurt because she'd humiliated him.

But mostly it hurt because she'd made a fool of him, using his own emotions against him. Why didn't she just cut out his heart with a letter opener?

She probably thought about that.

He'd bared his soul to the woman he knew as Unhappily Unwed. He'd opened up to her, as difficult as that had been for him to do with anyone since the divorce. He'd taken a chance, and Laura had made a fool of him.

In a major way.

And all the time, she was probably laughing at me, he thought miserably.

Probably? I'm sure she was!

All the things she said to him, all the sensitivity and sincerity—had it all been a put-on? Was it all just part of the game she'd been playing with him?

Why did she bother?

What do you think, chump?

How could he have been so stupid? he wondered now. How could he have fallen for all of it so easily? *That's an easy one. I was lonely. Lonely and dumb.*

Very, very dumb.

They tend to go hand in hand, don't they?

He glared at the computer again, wishing he'd stuck to his guns. Wishing he'd never bought the damn thing. Wishing he'd never checked out that network. Wishing he'd never opened Pandora's box.

Wishing he could forget.

Wishing he could have left Laura in the past, where she belonged.

Still in love with Ben?

What a ridiculous idea, Laura thought angrily. *What a completely, perfectly, incredibly ridiculous idea that was! Once was enough.* More than enough.

She wasn't in the habit of making the same mistake twice.

Why did Zara have to be so very perceptive? Why did she have to be so outspoken?

Laura felt so foolish, so very, very foolish at the moment. Just thinking about how open, how forthcoming she'd been with the man who called himself Misery Loves Company made her physically ill. He was probably having a good laugh over it at this very moment.

The jerk!

How could she have been so stupid?

How indeed? How could she have communicated with him for so long and on such an intimate level and *not* known who he was? How could he have so completely fooled her?

How could she have let her guard down?

How can I still be in love with him?

Foolish as she was, it was the truth. Zara was right, though Laura wasn't about to tell her so.

I am still in love with him.

Never in a million years would Laura ever admit to Zara that she still loved Ben.

She wouldn't have to. Zara *knew*.

And it'll be just as long before I go near a computer again—except for strictly professional reasons, she promised herself.

No more networks.

No more bulletin boards.

No more unidentified men.

And no more "blind dates," she thought, wishing now she'd not only agreed to exchange names, but insisted upon it before they met.

She could have saved herself a lot of embarrassment.

She could have told Ben where to go.

She could have avoided that scene at the restaurant, she realized.

She wouldn't have had to face him.

He wouldn't be laughing at her now.

She wouldn't be so miserable.

And she was sure he was laughing at her right now. She didn't doubt for a moment that her ex-husband was, at this very moment, getting his jollies at her expense.

She looked at the computer and saw Ben's face. It made her want to smash the screen. It made her want to trash the stupid thing.

No! she commanded herself. *You can't let him get to you.*

Forget about him.

He's not worth it.

He's really not.

But when she turned the lights out and went to bed, the computer was in the trash can.

12

I ought to, Ben was thinking.

I ought to do it. She deserves it.

He was staring at the computer, wondering if Laura had returned to the network, considering the possibility of setting her up, having some guy play up to her on-line the way she played up to him. That would be perfect, except for one thing.

Himself.

Only his own jealousy prevented him from carrying out that plan.

And he *was* jealous. No doubt about that. He could deny it to Sam and Ray; he could deny it to his mother—but no way could he deny it to himself. Sam had been right. He'd never really gotten over her. He probably never *would* get over her. She'd always be there, standing between him and whatever happiness might come his way.

Always. Always Laura.

He'd tried. Heaven knows he'd tried.

And failed.

The bottom line was that, like it or not, he still loved her. His feelings for her were as strong now as they'd ever been. He wished they weren't, but that was the reality. He couldn't just turn them off like a light switch. He couldn't even disconnect them—unfortunately.

He tried that, too.

It would have been easier for him if he could, he decided now. There was no future for him, not with her. He'd known that for a long time now. He'd known it since the day she went off to Chicago and he filed for divorce.

A divorce he'd never really wanted.

It would never work, he told himself.

Never in a million years.

Would it?

No...

He thought about it now, recalling the rapport that had existed between them while they were communicating via the network. Was it for real? He couldn't be sure, since he wasn't convinced the Laura on the network was in any way the *real* Laura.

She'd been putting him on—hadn't she?

Which one was the real Laura? he wondered. *The one I lived with all those years—or the one I just met?*

He'd been completely open with her as Misery Loves Company. He'd bared his soul to her on-line as he'd been unable to do face-to-face in those last few years of their marriage. He'd told her his innermost thoughts and feelings. Was it possible that she had done the same? Could it be—had she been straight with him?

Were her feelings for him genuine?

Was it possible that she really *didn't* know that he was Misery Loves Company? Was she as surprised as he had been?

Had the joke been on *both* of them?

Is it possible that I'm just a fool who's carrying a torch for a woman who chose a bank over me?

Or is this a second chance for us?

He wished he knew.

Laura was beginning to wonder whether she and Ben were throwing away a second chance.

She was having second thoughts. She was starting to wonder if she might have been wrong about Ben— about a lot of things. He'd been wrong about her—so it *was* possible that she could be wrong about him. Maybe he really *didn't* know she was Unhappily Unwed.

She smiled to herself. *He would make something of that,* she thought.

Could he really have been as surprised as he seemed at the restaurant?

If he didn't know it was her—and even if he did—if he *wasn't* putting her on, then all of those wonderful, caring things he said to her were genuine, straight-from-the-heart feelings. Beautiful, honest feelings— the kind she'd hope her husband would always have for her.

The kind she'd once hoped he had for her.

If that were true, it would mean there was still hope for them.

A chance. A slim one, but a chance nonetheless.

Is it possible? she asked herself.

Could he have been sincere?

She had to find out. But how?

Good question.

The logical answer was to go see him, talk to him. Drive to Fowler Falls, find him.

I couldn't, she told herself.

What if he wouldn't talk to her?

That was a definite possibility.

He might not. She'd never forget how angry he was that night at the restaurant, how furious he'd been when he saw her—

Furious! He'd been furious.

"Wait a minute!" she exclaimed, excited. "He was angry because he thought he'd been had! He *didn't* know it was me!"

That was no act.

He couldn't have, she thought. *And if he didn't, he believed I was a new woman in his life, someone he could be open and honest with.*

Open. Honest. The real Ben.

That, or he realized what a whale of a mistake he made with me and was telling this new woman what he thought she wanted to hear.

Surely not!

There's only one way I'm going to find out for sure.

She had to see him, talk to him.

She leaned across the desk and pressed the button on the intercom. "Zara, come in here, please," she said.

"Right away, boss."

Less than a minute later, Zara came through the door. "What's up?" she wanted to know.

"I have to leave early." *Like now,* she was thinking.

"Like when?"

Was she a mind reader, or what? "Like right now."

"Okay if I ask where you're going?"

"Fowler Falls."

If Zara was surprised, she concealed it well.

"When will you be back?"

Laura thought about it. "I have no idea."

"Go talk to her," Sam urged.

Easier said than done, little brother.

"And say what?" Ben wanted to know.

"Tell her you still love her. Tell her you want her back!" Sam told him. "Tell her what a fool you've been."

And wait for her to slam the door in my face. Ben raised an eyebrow. "Thanks."

"Well, you have been."

"Even if I have, I don't particularly like to be reminded of it," Ben grumbled. *I do enough of that myself.*

"No, but maybe it's just what you need," Sam suggested.

"Meaning what?" *Meaning a building has to fall on me or something.*

"Meaning maybe you need to be reminded not to make the same mistake twice."

"No, little brother," Ben said, shaking his head. "I *don't* need to be reminded."

Sam wasn't convinced. "So why don't you go see her, then? You obviously want to."

"It's not that simple." *Not by a long shot.*

"Why not?"

"What if she refused to see me?" *Which she probably would.*

"You'll never know unless you give it a shot," Sam pointed out.

True. "I don't exactly enjoy having doors slammed in my face," Ben admitted.

"Do you enjoy being alone?"

"What kind of question is that?" Ben asked, irritated.

"An honest one. Do you?"

Hardly. "What is this?" Ben wanted to know. "It wasn't all that long ago that you were telling me to go out and meet someone and get over Laura." *In fact, it was just last week.*

"That would have been great if you had," Sam said, "but if it hadn't worked out, at least it would have given you something to think about."

It did. "How so?"

"It could have helped you sort out your feelings for Laura."

Wrong. It made matters worse. "Right." *Tell him what he wants to hear. Maybe he'll go away.*

"But then, you seem to have been sure of those feelings all along," Sam went on, reminding him of things he didn't particularly want to be reminded of.

Go away, Sam.

Ben didn't respond.

Go away, Sam.

"Well, are you or aren't you?"

"Are I or aren't I what?" This was becoming tiresome.

"Going to Chicago."

You bet I am.

He thought about it for a moment. "Yes. I am." He tossed Sam the keys to the garage. "Lock up for me, will you?" he called over his shoulder as he headed for the exit.

They'd probably close up before he reached the city limits, but he didn't care.

Sam grinned. "You bet!"

Soon, Laura told herself.

There was almost no traffic on the two-lane highway leading to Fowler Falls. The sun was setting, and Laura felt as though she'd been on the road all day rather than a little over an hour and a half. Was she that anxious? Was that why it seemed to be taking longer than it normally did?

Was she that anxious?

Not much longer, she thought as she checked her watch. Another forty-five minutes and she'd be in Fowler Falls. Another forty-five minutes and she'd be face-to-face with Ben.

Again.

For better or worse.

Laura sighed heavily. Bad choice of words.

She wondered how he'd react when he saw her. *Well, Ben,* she thought, *I'll be there soon. Will you be glad to see me, or will I go back to Chicago with the imprint of a screen door on my face?*

She wondered.

She had no idea what to expect. The last time she saw him, he'd looked at her in a way that indicated if he never saw her again, it would be too soon. He'd looked at her as if he hated her, as he could kill her with his bare hands.

For a minute there, she'd thought he might.

Does he still feel that way?

She'd soon find out.

She wished she could be sure. She was taking a chance, going to Fowler Falls like this. What if he didn't want to see her? What if he refused to talk to her? What if it was too late for her, for them?

She couldn't think about that now.

How did it ever come to this? she asked herself. *Ben and I used to be so close. There was a time when we told each other everything, when each of us knew what the other was thinking and feeling.* A time when she honestly believed they would last forever.

That their love would last forever.

Now she had no idea what to expect.

She wished she did.

It was going to be a long night.

A very long night.

Ben switched his headlights on. Only a half hour out of Fowler Falls and it was dark already. It would be at least another hour and a half before he reached Chicago, and maybe another fifteen minutes to her apartment.

He could only hope she would be there.

If I get past her doorman, Ben thought. *No guarantees there.*

He couldn't be sure she'd even see him.

He found himself recalling another time, a happier time, when he didn't have to wonder what Laura was feeling or how she might react. *We were so in tune to each other then,* he thought. *We had everything in common.*

Or so he'd thought.

What went wrong?

Was it his fault?

Maybe it's not too late. Maybe the relationship— our relationship—can still be saved.

Maybe we can go back, after all.

His thoughts were interrupted by a loud noise that suddenly arose from his engine—followed almost immediately by its sudden death. Coasting the truck to the shoulder of the road, he muttered angrily under his breath and got out to check under the hood. This was, he decided, the worst possible time for something to go wrong.

Just what I don't need, he thought. *Stuck out here in the middle of the night—well, maybe not the middle of the night, but close enough—with a dead motor, no garage for miles and not a motorist in sight.*

I shouldn't have resisted the idea of getting a car phone.

Laura saw the flashing lights as she approached. *Looks like somebody's in trouble,* she thought. *What a place to get stranded.*

Laura knew better than to stop for a motorist who appeared to have broken down, especially at night on a deserted road—but she could summon help on her car phone. These days, much as one might want to, it just wasn't safe to stop. Being a Good Samaritan often—too often—meant you ended up a *dead* Samaritan.

Unfortunately.

But as she reached for her car phone, she stopped short, recognizing the pickup truck. *That's Ben's truck,* she thought. What was he doing out here, like this, at this time of night?

Coming to a slow stop, she rolled down her window. "Ben?"

He raised his head from his position under the hood. "Laura?" he asked, surprised. "What are you doing out here?"

She hesitated momentarily. "I was coming to see you," she finally confessed, getting out of the car.

Ben started to laugh hysterically.

"What's so funny about that?" Laura asked, feeling more than a little hurt.

"I was on my way to Chicago to see you!" he told her.

Coming to see me?

Then she started to laugh, too.

Does that mean—? "From the time I left Chicago, I had these visions of you slamming the door in my face," she admitted.

"I didn't think I'd even get that far at your place." He laughed.

"Oh—you mean the doorman?"

"Lurch." It was the first time he'd ever told her he compared her burly doorman to the Addams Family's creepy butler. She tried not to laugh—unsuccessfully.

"You call him *Lurch?*" Laura laughed even harder.

Ben nodded. "There's a resemblance, don't you think?"

"Now that you mention it..."

He was right.

"Why were you coming to see me?" he asked then.

Do I tell him the truth? "To ask you something."

"What?"

Do I tell him the truth? she asked herself again. "I wanted to find out if you really meant all the things you said on the network," she answered honestly. "You?"

He looked a little embarrassed. "Pretty much the same thing."

"Did you?" she asked.

"What?"

"Mean the things you said?"

This time he didn't hesitate. "Every word," he said. "What about you?"

She nodded.

"It would seem we suffered from a real failure to communicate," he said.

"Definitely."

"I never knew you felt the way you did."

"I was pretty surprised by some of the feelings you expressed, too," she said.

"We just stopped listening to each other, I guess."

"It would seem we would have been better off if we hadn't grown up."

"In some ways, anyway."

"Was I really so inconsiderate of your feelings?" she wanted to know.

"Most of the time. Me?"

She nodded.

Then they both started to laugh again.

Laura leaned against the front of the truck, ignoring the grease and grime that would probably ruin her dove-gray suit. "I've never really stopped loving you, Ben," she confessed. "Never, no matter what."

His eyes met hers in the darkness. "I didn't want the divorce," he said quietly. "It was the hardest thing I've ever had to do."

"Do you still love me?"

"As much as I ever have." He took her in his arms. "I hope it's not too late for us."

"It isn't if we don't want it to be."

"That simple, is it?" She shook her head.

"Not simple at all. We've still got a lot of baggage to deal with," he acknowledged. "But if we want it, we can do it."

"I want it."

"So do I."

He kissed her then, a long, lingering kiss that she returned eagerly.

"Will you marry me?" he asked.

"Again?"

"Again."

"You bet!"

"Is that a yes?"

"That's a yes. That's definitely a yes."

It started to rain then—not a light summer shower, but a hard, driving rain. Neither of them moved right away, just held each other tightly in the downpour, hugging and kissing.

"I guess we should get in the car," Laura said finally.

"I guess we should."

They got in—but in the back seat, not the front. "You can use the car phone to call a tow truck," she told him.

"Not yet."

She raised an eyebrow. "Embarrassed?"

"About what?"

"Having a garage and not being able to get your own truck started." She giggled.

"I don't work on motors," he told her. "I work on bodies."

And then he proved it.

Epilogue

It was, without a doubt, the most unique wedding any of the guests had ever witnessed.

The bride didn't wear white. Or maybe she did.

No one could be sure because none of the guests were in the same room with the bride. They all wondered if the groom was.

No one knew for sure.

The ceremony was performed on-line. Even the minister was on-line. All of the guests were on-line. The guests, none of whom had ever met either the bride or the groom, were scattered all over the continental United States.

A "Cyberwedding," they called it.

The wire services picked it up. The headlines read The Bride Wore Software.

The real wedding, which took place in Fowler Falls the next week, was an even bigger event, though it received no media coverage. Only the close friends and family members who were there for the candlelight ceremony in the little church on the edge of town knew what a major event this wedding really was.

It had been a long time coming.

No one in Fowler Falls had ever doubted for a minute that, one day, Ben and Laura would get together again. Everyone who knew them believed in the power of their love.

Only Ben and Laura had stopped believing—and then only for a little while. It was a mistake they vowed never to make again. Literally. They included it in the marriage vows they'd written themselves.

"Where are we going?" Laura asked as they drove off on their honeymoon.

"I told you, it's a surprise," Ben answered, grinning.

"You won't even give me a hint?"

"Nope."

"Not even a little one?"

"Nope."

"Why not?"

"Because it's a surprise," he told her again.

"A hint—just a vague little hint—wouldn't hurt," she said, pressuring him.

"Yes, it would," he insisted.

"How so?"

"I'm not going to tell you."

"Ben!"

"You might as well give up, sweetheart," he told her. "You're not going to have a clue until we get there." She would never guess that they were going to Italy.

"That's not fair!" She gave him a playful poke.

"Sure it is," he said with a chuckle. "You know the saying— 'all's fair in love and war.'"

"Well, at least this isn't war," she said gratefully.

Ben nodded. "Not anymore, anyway."

"How could we have been so blind?" Laura questioned.

"Beats me."

"Think we'll be able to live up to our vows this time around?" she wondered aloud.

"I don't have a crystal ball or anything like that," he said, turning his eyes from the road for a moment, "but I, for one, intend to work like hell at it."

"That makes two of us," Laura said. "I'm never going to let my work come between us again."

"That, my love, will be impossible," he told her.

She looked at him. "What makes you say that?" she asked, suddenly concerned that he might not have the same faith in her that she had in him.

"The realities, sweetheart," he said. "You've got a demanding position, a lot of responsibility—and you work in Chicago."

"I could always come back to the bank in Fowler Falls," she suggested.

He shook his head. "I made that mistake before."

"Mistake?"

"Forcing you to choose between me and your career," he said. "No more. I'm not out to change you, Laura. I love you just the way you are—career and all." Even if that meant only having weekends most of the time.

"But will you always feel that way?" she asked dubiously. "A commuter marriage won't be easy."

"I didn't say it would always be easy." He drew her close. "But I love you and I want you to be happy. I'd rather have fewer hours with you then twenty-four hours a day with any other woman."

She kissed him. "I *will* have to take some time off," she said.

"Vacations, sure."

"No—maternity leave."

He slammed on the brakes. The car skidded to a stop. "Maternity leave?" he asked. "You're not—"

She laughed. "Not yet—but I'm working on it."

He laughed, too. This was one job he wasn't going to mind putting in a *lot* of overtime to accomplish.

In fact, he was looking forward to it.

*   *   *   *   *

Silhouette

SPECIAL EDITION

SPECIAL EDITION

Stories of love and life, these powerful
novels are tales that you can identify with—
romances with "something special" added in!

Fall in love with the stories of authors such
as **Nora Roberts, Diana Palmer, Ginna Gray**
and many more of your special favorites—as
well as wonderful new voices!

Special Edition brings you
entertainment for the heart!

SSE-GEN

SILHOUETTE®

Desire®

Do you want...

Dangerously handsome heroes

Evocative, everlasting love stories

Sizzling and tantalizing sensuality

Incredibly sexy miniseries like **MAN OF THE MONTH**

Red-hot romance

Enticing entertainment that can't be beat!

You'll find all of this, and much *more* each and
every month in **SILHOUETTE DESIRE**. Don't miss these
unforgettable love stories by some of romance's hottest
authors. Silhouette Desire—where your fantasies will
always come true....

DES-GEN

INTIMATE MOMENTS®
Silhouette®

If you've got the time...
We've got the
INTIMATE MOMENTS

Passion. Suspense. Desire. Drama. Enter a world
that's larger than life, where men and women
overcome life's greatest odds for the ultimate prize:
love. Nonstop excitement is closer than you
think...in Silhouette Intimate Moments!

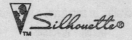
Silhouette®

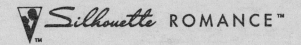

Silhouette ROMANCE™

What's a single dad to do when he needs a wife
by next Thursday?

Who's a confirmed bachelor to call when he finds a
baby on his doorstep?

How does a plain Jane in love with her gorgeous boss
get him to notice her?

From classic love stories to romantic comedies to emotional heart
tuggers, **Silhouette Romance** offers six irresistible novels every
month by some of your favorite authors!
Such as...beloved bestsellers **Diana Palmer,**
Annette Broadrick, Suzanne Carey, Elizabeth August
and **Marie Ferrarella**, to name just a few—and some sure to
become favorites!

Fabulous Fathers...Bundles of Joy...Miniseries...
Months of blushing brides and convenient weddings...
Holiday celebrations... You'll find all this and much more in
Silhouette Romance—always emotional, always enjoyable,
always about love!

SR-GEN

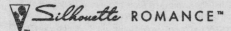

SILHOUETTE... Where Passion Lives

Don't miss these Silhouette favorites by some of our most distinguished authors! And now you can receive a discount by ordering two or more titles!

SD#05849	MYSTERY LADY by Jackie Merritt	$2.99	☐
SD#05867	THE BABY DOCTOR	$2.99 U.S.	☐
	by Peggy Moreland	$3.50 CAN.	☐
IM#07610	SURROGATE DAD	$3.50 U.S.	☐
	by Marion Smith Collins	$3.99 CAN.	☐
IM#07616	EYEWITNESS	$3.50 U.S.	☐
	by Kathleen Creighton	$3.99 CAN.	☐
SE#09934	THE ADVENTURER	$3.50 U.S.	☐
	by Diana Whitney	$3.99 CAN.	☐
SE#09916	AN INTERRUPTED MARRIAGE	$3.50 U.S.	☐
	by Laurey Bright	$3.99 CAN.	☐
SR#19050	MISS SCROOGE	$2.75 U.S.	☐
	by Toni Collins	$3.25 CAN.	☐
SR#08994	CALEB'S SON	$2.75	☐
	by Laurie Paige		
YT#52001	WANTED: PERFECT PARTNER	$3.50 U.S.	☐
	by Debbie Macomber	$3.99 CAN.	☐
YT#52002	LISTEN UP, LOVER	$3.50 U.S.	☐
	by Lori Herter	$3.99 CAN.	☐
	(limited quantities available on certain titles)		

TOTAL AMOUNT	$_____
DEDUCT: **10% DISCOUNT FOR 2+ BOOKS**	$_____
POSTAGE & HANDLING	$_____
($1.00 for one book, 50¢ for each additional)	
APPLICABLE TAXES**	$_____
TOTAL PAYABLE	$_____
(check or money order—please do not send cash)	

To order, send the completed form with your name, address, zip or postal code, along with a check or money order for the total above, payable to Silhouette Books, to: **In the U.S.:** 3010 Walden Avenue, P.O. Box 9077, Buffalo, NY 14269-9077; **In Canada:** P.O. Box 636, Fort Erie, Ontario, L2A 5X3.

Name:_____

Address:_____City:_____

State/Prov.:_____ Zip/Postal Code:_____

**New York residents remit applicable sales taxes.
  Canadian residents remit applicable GST and provincial taxes.   SBACK-MM2

Silhouette®